Br... the ...
Summer

Also by Julia Green

Breathing Underwater
Drawing with Light
Blue Moon
Baby Blue
Hunter's Heart

Bringing the Summer

JULIA GREEN

LONDON BERLIN NEW YORK SYDNEY

First published in Great Britain in May 2012 by
Bloomsbury Publishing Plc
50 Bedford Square, London, WC1B 3DP

A CIP catalogue record for this book is available
from the British Library

ISBN 978 1 4088 1958 6

Typeset by Hewer Text UK Ltd, Edinburgh
Printed in Great Britain by Clays Ltd, St Ives Plc, Bungay, Suffolk

1 3 5 7 9 10 8 6 4 2

www.bloomsbury.com
www.julia-green.co.uk

For Jesse and Jack

One

It's the end of August, my last day on the island of St Ailla.

'I'm just going out,' I call to Evie as I slip out of the back door, on my way to the shed to pick up my wetsuit. 'One final swim!'

'Keep an eye on the time, Freya,' she calls back from the kitchen. 'The ferry leaves at eleven.'

I run down the lane past the farm to the campsite, turn left through the wooden gate into the field, up the earthy track between flowering gorse bushes that smell like coconut. At the top of Wind Down I stop like I always do at the turf maze; I walk carefully round the ridged path into the middle and back out again. It's part of my ritual of saying goodbye.

I turn into the wind and start running over the short grass towards Beady Pool. There's no one here. I peel off my clothes, wriggle into my wetsuit. The water is freezing even though the sun's out today, the sea a brilliant turquoise. I swim out, overarm, as far as the end of the line of rock, and then back, more slowly, breaststroke. This is the last time I'll swim in the sea this year. I turn on to my back and let myself float, arms outstretched, eyes open to the wide blue sky. For a moment I let myself drift, held by the water, surrounded by light.

Finally, when it's time to go, Evie and Gramps walk me down to the jetty. *Spirit*, the small island boat, is already waiting to take passengers over to Main Island for the ferry. Evie and Gramps hold me between them for a long goodbye hug.

'Take care, sweetheart,' Gramps says. 'Come back to see us soon.' He wipes his eyes with his sleeve. 'You're leaving with the swallows, Freya.' He points to the row of birds lined up along the telephone wire at the top of the jetty.

'They're just practising,' Evie tells him. 'They're not going yet. They're not quite ready for that long journey south.' She squeezes his hand. 'And they'll be back next year, even the young ones. Straight back to the nests where they were born.'

She hugs me one last time. 'It's been so lovely having you here all summer it's hard to let you go!' She laughs. 'But you know what they say: one door shuts and another one opens!'

I find a seat at the back of the boat, like I always do, so I can watch my grandparents getting smaller and smaller, and the gap of sea between us stretching bigger and wider. I wave until they are tiny dots, and then I turn and I face the other way, looking forward.

It's as if I've got two lives, my island life, and my

normal one, back on the mainland. This is the moment when I cross over, one to the other. It's always hard. But it's like Evie says: another door opening. The beginning of something new.

Two

The train's packed. At each station, more people pile in. The luggage racks are spilling over with bags and beach stuff, surfboards propped up at the end of the carriage. The over-breathed air is thick with the smell of suntan lotion on hot skin. I'm pressed in the window seat in Coach A, the quiet carriage at the front of the train, my book open on the table before me unread, just wanting to be home, now. There's still at least two and a half hours to go.

A sudden jolt shakes the train, followed by the stink of brakes as the train judders to a long-drawn-out stop. For a moment, everyone is silent. It feels as if the train might tip over. Are we about to crash? I am suddenly deeply afraid, alert to danger even though nothing else happens: the train simply stops. The acrid smell of the too-hard braking seeps through the train.

The train manager's voice comes over the intercom: a man's voice, kind and oddly human, shocked by his own words which come out in a rush and say too much, too soon: 'Someone's walked out on to the line!' before he reverts to the usual train-manager language: 'There has been a fatality. There will be a severe delay to your journey.'

A babble of voices. All around me, people start getting their phones out, as if desperate to speak, to tell someone close to them. They repeat the exact same words: *someone walked out on to the line . . . fatality . . . delay.* The woman opposite me tuts. 'It's the driver you feel sorry for.'

I look out of the window. Because I'm in the front carriage, I can see it all unfold. The train manager struggles into a bright orange vest, talking into his phone at the same time. Another man joins him. The manager steps back on to the train and his voice comes again, over the loudspeaker system: 'Could the relief driver who is travelling on this train please come forward, and bring two cups of tea for the drivers from the buffet as you come through.'

The little detail of the cups of tea brings the tragedy horribly into focus. I can imagine everything, of course: the driver, traumatised, needs his sweet tea. He won't be allowed to drive the train. In my too vivid imagination, already tuned into death and disaster, I'm with him in the front of the train as he sees the person step out, as he applies the brakes, as he closes his eyes, because it takes *miles* for a train at that speed to stop and there is nothing, nothing he can do . . .

The driver climbs down from the cab, and the manager moves over to stand beside him. Two of the three men light cigarettes. A man holding two paper cups of tea walks slowly through our carriage and everyone goes quiet again, watching. He joins the men at the side of the track. The drivers sip tea. They've got their backs to the train; I can't see their faces.

We wait. People talk. A girl on the other side of the train carriage says she saw something fly past the window; she'd thought it was just a piece of wood, but now she thinks it was a shoe, or something . . .

Another announcement. 'We apologise for the severe delay to your journey this afternoon. British Transport Police have now arrived.'

I text Mum to say my train's going to be really late. I don't tell her why. She texts me back. **Can you get a taxi from the station? Dad and I have to go out. Sorry. See u later. Love Mum xx**

A policeman turns up. He writes things down in a notebook, nodding. I take in more details of the driver; grey hair, a beard, middle-aged, blue short-sleeved shirt, railway uniform. The other men seem to be looking after him, in their particularly male way: cigarettes, a joke, even; standing very close without actually touching.

The policeman pulls on latex gloves. He walks away, and I imagine him picking things up . . . pieces up . . . my mind shuts down then. I'm trying not to think about what might be left, scattered along the track or caught under the wheels . . .

'We have nothing further to report. We apologise for the severe delay to your journey. Engineers are still inspecting the train for any damage caused by the incident.'

The idea that the *train* might be damaged . . . My brain reels.

Even as it happens, I see what I'm doing. It's as if I'm noting everything down, committing the details to memory, as if I might be called upon as a witness, later. Or is it my own way of keeping the real truths at a distance, so I don't feel anything?

Eventually – an hour, maybe an hour and a half later – the train limps slowly into the next station. We all have to get off. The platform's crowded with people: trains delayed in either direction; no one going anywhere.

I stand, almost dizzy, on the platform with my bag, and I do not mean to, but I do see the front of the train, and the huge dent. I hug myself and weep.

I suppose I am attuned to death, and grief, and the tragic moment that splits the world in two. It happened in my own family, when my brother, Joe, died in a boating accident at the island I've just travelled from. Bit by bit, we've pieced our lives together again, and that's not what I want to write about now, because I did all that two years ago, when I was fourteen, and that's all over. But I suppose, thinking about it now, it's why the death of an unknown person under the wheels of the train I just *happened* to be travelling on, wouldn't leave me alone. I kept thinking about it, and wondering *why*, and wondering *who*.

Three

The house feels empty, as if nothing has disturbed the air for hours. The table is tidy, the draining board clean, the polished wooden floor swept. Through the back window the garden is green and gold in the late evening sunlight. It's taken me almost nine hours to get home. I pick up the note on the table. *Dear Freya . . . We've gone out for dinner but look forward to seeing you tonight when we get back, or in the morning if you've already gone to bed . . .*

Maybe it's better like this. I won't go blurting out what happened, now. There's no point raking up old sadness, which is what happens whenever you mention another horrible thing. Mum still can't watch certain things on telly. She won't watch the news, because it is too likely to bring up awful tragic events: children dying, random acts of unbelievable cruelty. Dad's different: he has put all his energy into making our new house really beautiful. It's almost finished: polished wooden floors, huge windows, open-plan kitchen/dining/sitting room, full of light.

I'm too exhausted to cook anything for my supper. I go upstairs and run a bath. I lie in the water watching the light drain from the sky as the sun sets. The silence of the house soothes me, little by little. In my bedroom, I find my bed made up with a clean white sheet, white duvet cover, white pillowcases. Someone – Mum, I guess – has placed a jug of pink and cream roses from the garden on the bedside table. I don't unpack.

Some time later, the sound of the front door opening startles me awake. I listen to their voices drifting upstairs, but I'm too drowsy to get up. The familiar noises of my parents getting ready for bed, running a bath, lull me back towards sleep. At one point, footsteps pad along the landing and I know Mum's standing outside my room, looking through the small gap in the barely open door, checking I'm safe. She stays a while, and then, satisfied, she pads back again.

I'm breathing deeply, steadily, like you do when you're almost asleep. And then, just as I'm drifting off properly, I feel again the jolt in my body, like on the train, except it's as if it's me, falling.

The moment of *impact*.

Solid train meeting soft flesh.

Next morning, after breakfast together, me telling the story of my island summer, answering questions about Gramps and Evie, after all that, and once Mum and Dad have both left for work, I turn on my computer. I check emails.

I flick through local news items, to see if there's anything about yesterday's accident. Nothing. But as soon as I type the two words *train suicides* into the search engine, a whole load of references come up: far too many. I'm suddenly sickened by the whole business, can't bear to read any of them.

I make coffee, instead, and take it with me into the garden, to the place we've made for remembering Joe. I sit on the bench, under the cream roses, and I doodle in my sketchbook for a while. I flip back through the last few pages, full of six weeks' worth of drawings: summer on St Ailla. Boats at the jetty; the old lighthouse; the beach at Beady Pool; Danny fishing for mackerel off the rocks. Danny's my friend who I first met three summers ago when he was staying with his family at the farm campsite, down the lane from Evie and Gramps' house. I've seen him each summer since. Except this year, because it rained so much, they went home early.

I send him a quick text. **Back home now :(You missed the best days. Sunny all this week! Fx**

In a week's time I shall be starting college. I'm going to be doing my A levels at the further education college in town: Art, English and Biology. Miranda will be there, too. Miranda and I have been best friends for ever.

I phone her. She doesn't answer, so I text her instead. **I'm back! Want 2 meet up 2day? I'm going to swim at the weir. See you there at 2? Bring a picnic.**

It's the lazy end of summer, just before everything changes. Sometimes it's a sad time of year for us (Joe died in late August) but this year I'm ready for change, for a new beginning. It's been a wetter than usual summer, but the last week has been fine and sunny: what Dad calls an Indian summer. One that comes late and unexpectedly.

The field next to the river where you can swim above the weir is the closest thing we've got to a beach in this landlocked city. On hot days, local kids cycle there along the towpath that runs next to the canal. Families come too.

I haven't ridden my bike all summer. I find it at the back of the garage, covered in dust and spiders' webs and with a flat tyre. It takes me ages to find a bike pump. I can't be bothered to mend a puncture now so I just pump up the tyre and hope for the best. I put the bike pump in the bag with the picnic food, just in case.

It's easier cycling once I'm off the road and on to the level towpath. I've forgotten how good it feels, spinning along past the moored-up boats, past the backs of houses and long gardens, ducking under the stone bridges that cross the canal. It doesn't take long before I've left the city way behind and the houses have given way to fields. I reach the place where you have to come off the path and take a track down to a lane and the level crossing over the railway. I lock the bike up against the fence, where there are already loads of other bikes, pick up my bag and push through the wicket gate.

Wait. Watch. Listen, the wooden sign says. It's a clear stretch of railway so you can see easily whether there's a train coming either way, and there's a proper crossing, wooden boards over the rails, so it's perfectly safe. Today more than usual I take in the other sign: *Danger of Death*. It's totally silent. No humming of the rails, no train remotely in view either direction. I know that the London train comes through every half-hour, and there are slower local trains every so often. Even so, I wait, and listen again, before I walk across. My palms are sweaty by the time I've got to the other side, through the gate and across the stile into the field.

The cows have retreated to the opposite end of the field, mostly lying down at the edge under trees. The sound of splashing water and shouting voices drifts up from the river. I can't see Miranda. I wander through the groups of people sunbathing on the grass till I see people I recognise from school. Ellie and Tabitha wave at me. I go over to them.

'All right?' Ellie says.

'Yes. You?'

She nods, sleepily.

Tabby gets up and gives me a hug. 'You look great, Freya! Good summer?'

'Amazing!' I say. 'You?'

She shrugs. 'Nothing special.' She looks at my rolled-up towel. 'You swimming?'

I nod. 'You'll be staying a while? I'll leave my stuff here.' I strip off my skirt and top – I've got my swimming things on already, underneath – and walk over the grass towards the river. I climb down the steep bank to the water.

Compared to the sea, the river water's almost warm. I wade in further and as soon as it's deep enough, start swimming upstream away from the line of kids splashing at the edge and balancing along the top of the weir. The light is golden, streaming through a canopy of green willow branches, making liquid gold on the surface of the river as it flows downstream. I swim against the current with strong, smooth overarm strokes until I'm far upstream and there's no one else around.

Swimming in a river is very different from the sea. The way it moves, and the colour; even the texture of the water is different, like silk, soft against my skin instead of stinging and salty. I keep away from the bank, where the water is shallow and it's easy to stir up silt with your feet. A kingfisher flashes across in front of me, and disappears again. Suddenly hungry, I tread water and turn, swim back downstream.

I find Miranda sitting on the weir, her legs dangling over the edge. Her skin is smooth and golden, her hair sun-bleached from two weeks of Spanish sun.

'Hey, you!'

She turns. 'Freya!'

We hug, and she shivers. 'You're freezing! How long have you been in the water?'

'Long enough. I'm hungry. Coming out?'

She walks carefully back along the slippery edge. The weed beneath the water looks like combed green hair. I swim beside her until it's too shallow, clamber out on to the bank and walk after her, dripping, to my towel. When I've dried myself, I spread out the cotton sheet I've brought for us to lie on, and we share our picnics.

The afternoon wears on, a drowsy, hot September day, wasps buzzing lazily round the bags and bottles, Miranda and me catching up on a whole summer apart. Some of the time, we just doze in the sun. Warmed through, contented, I listen to Miranda's account of summer love in Spain, the hopelessness of holiday romance. Someone called Jamie.

'So I probably won't see him ever again!' She sighs.

'Where does he live?'

'Edinburgh. Well, that's where he's studying.'

'You could fly,' I say. 'From Bristol.'

'It wouldn't be the same, though,' Miranda says. 'It only worked because of where we were.'

'Well then.'

'Perhaps I'll meet someone at college. There might be boys we don't know.'

'Of course there will. Loads of new people.'

'And Danny? How did that go?' Miranda asks me.

'Good. Only I didn't see much of him. They left early. It was wet almost all the time he was there.'

'And?'

'Nothing else. Nothing to report.'

Miranda narrows her eyes. 'Are you sure?'

'Promise.'

'OK. I believe you. I think.'

I laugh. Miranda's always trying to matchmake. It's her main occupation. She's never even met Danny, but she's convinced he'd be perfect for me, if only he was about a year older. At our age, she says, girls are sooo much more mature than boys. Danny's sixteen, like me.

By seven, most of the families have packed up and gone home and a new load of people arrive, with barbecues and beer and music. Swallows swoop low over the field, catching flies. As the sun goes down, the sky turns pink and golden and then a deep turquoise blue. We're both chilled from sitting still so long. The cows that were grazing at the far end of the field move closer towards the river, chomping the dampening grass as they go.

I stand up and stretch. 'Better go back. I haven't got proper lights on my bike.'

We pack up the picnic things, and say goodbye to the people we know from school, and traipse back up the path to the railway crossing. There aren't so many bikes piled up now. We unlock ours and disentangle them.

By the time we start cycling back, side by side along the canal towpath, the boat people are sitting in groups round small fires along the grass at the edge of the path, lanterns hanging on the low tree branches, and the summer night smells of wood smoke and roll-ups and charred meat.

'Would you like to live like that?' Miranda asks. 'On one of those narrowboats?'

'I wouldn't mind,' I say, 'in summer. Except, if I had a boat, I'd want to be able to go places. Not just on the canal, up and down.'

And that makes me think of my brother, who was

going to go places too. And then that reminds me of the train *incident*, so I tell Miranda about what happened, and it changes the mood of the evening, but not in a good way.

Miranda looks at me. 'You want to be careful,' she says. 'It was just a random thing. It didn't mean anything. Don't go brooding about it.'

'No,' I agree.

But of course I do. I just don't tell her about it any more.

Four

We're into the third week of college. It's mid-September, and the Indian summer is still with us: one sunny day after another. It's a waste, having to be inside so much. But at least college is different from school: you don't have registration with your tutor in the morning, or have to stay on the premises at breaks; you're free to come and go, and they treat you like you're grown up. Because the college is right in the middle of town, we can go off for coffees and lunch, and to the park, whenever we don't have lessons.

The art studios are amazing, much better than the school art rooms, and one of our teachers – we're supposed to call them lecturers, now, and we can use their first names (Jeanette) – is a proper successful artist who has exhibitions and sells her paintings. So it feels more real, and more as if it's a proper thing to do, instead of some *pipe dream*, which is what Dad thinks. One of my assignments is to research artists' interpretations of the theme of discord, so that's what I'm doing now, in the learning resources centre. It's the end of the day, and no one else is here.

It's only a few clicks on a search engine to go from Ana Mendieta and Annette Messager to Railway-Related Deaths. I'm searching, again, for something about the train accident.

I find a list of deaths, in date order. I check the places, and the dates. It's that simple. The stark details come up on the screen. The date, first, and the place. I find a name. *Bridie.* Immediately, my heart does a sort of leap. A real person, a girl, and she died. Of course she did. I knew that, didn't I? How could anyone possibly survive being hit by a train? But knowing the name, knowing it was a girl, makes it all suddenly much more shocking.

I find another article, from a local newspaper. There's just been an inquest in Exeter. It gives the date for the funeral, and the place. I look that up, too. I do all this research on autopilot, and I write it down in my notebook, as if it's part of the Art project. Perhaps in some weird way it is. I don't tell anyone. Bit by bit, I work out what I'm going to do. I don't tell anyone about that, either.

Five days later, I'm taking the train westwards again, on a Friday lunchtime. It means I'm skipping an English class, but . . . well, I couldn't explain to anyone why, but I just know I need to go to the girl's – Bridie's – funeral. It's at some random church in the middle of the city but the train journey is easy enough, and the church is only a short walk away, according to the street map I download.

It's the first time I've been on a train since it happened. I notice how much more nervous I am; the way I check out the other people in the carriage, and listen out to the different sounds of the engine. I breathe deeply to make myself relax. The train stops three times. A few people get on and off. No one takes any notice of me in my window seat with my notebook on the table in front of me.

At Exeter I get off the train and make my way out of the station and on to the main road. I check the map. I've allowed too much time: there's ages before I need to be there, so I walk along the main road to find a café. I choose one near the church, push open the door and go in.

I take in the black-and-white lino floor and a random collection of old wooden tables. I sit down at a sewing machine trestle table with metal legs. The café walls are papered with music sheets – pages of them from old books. I order tea. I do my usual thing of watching everyone come in and out. I draw; quick pen and ink sketches, and the sounds of the busy café waft over me: the hiss of the milk steamer; the clatter of cups and saucers; people chatting. I make my tea last a long time. I make up stories in my head about who people are, and why they're here. A mother and daughter: shopping trip. Three students, having a late lunch, planning some music event. An older man with a younger one – his son, who he hardly ever sees? I watch a middle-aged man and a woman leaning across the table to be closer, so rapt and intent on each other I guess they are new lovers. Not married. Perhaps it is the beginning of an affair . . .

The bell on the door jangles as a whole bunch of people come in. All part of one big family, I guess: the parents, then two grown-up daughters, two teenage boys and two babies. Apart from the babies, they're all dressed up really smartly, in black suits and polished black shoes, and the women have hats and even gloves and handbags, all black. They look totally out of place. But they come in anyway and people move chairs so they can all get round one table, and they're all laughing. I can't take my eyes off them.

I look down at my own clothes: jeans, a white shirt with little pearl buttons, short black jacket.

The family order coffees and cakes, and the babies – toddlers, really – squirm and whine, and one of the boys – he looks about eighteen – entertains them by folding paper serviettes to create animals: paper frogs that hop. The boy looks vaguely familiar, with his fair curly hair, and blue eyes, and hands with fine, long fingers. When he smiles, his face glows. At one point he looks directly at me, and I turn away, quickly. I bury myself in my drawings, shading in the background, adding a detail to the chair.

I check the time. Five more minutes.

The church is an ugly modern building. A small group of people are waiting outside. Everyone looks a bit shabby, and disconnected, as if they don't know each other. I hover, not knowing what to do now I'm here. I don't want to speak to anyone, or draw attention to myself. I'd expected just to slide into a pew at the back of the church. But when I'd imagined it, I suppose I was thinking of the sort of packed church we had for my brother, not this sparse gathering. And I feel a fraud, far worse than gatecrashing a party. A hanger-on, an intruder at someone else's tragedy.

The priest comes to the door and invites people in. I follow. I can't sit at the back now: there are so few people it would look even more obvious. So I slip in at the end of a row near two older women. It's horrible that there are so few people here, and terribly sad. The music starts, and then there's a sudden flurry of activity – more people arriving – and I look round to see that same family, the one from the café, file in to the pews behind me. The smart black clothes make sense, now. But they look out of place even here in church, because no one else is dressed in black, or even half as smart. It's a mystery, what connection they have with everyone else, or with the short life the priest is talking about, in his droning, churchy voice. *Our sister*, he calls her, but she isn't anyone's real sister as far as I can see.

What was I hoping to find out? Something about Bridie, I suppose, that might help me understand *why* she did what she did. But I don't find anything out from the priest's speech, which is bland, and general, as if he's never met the girl. He probably hasn't. There's no one at the front of the church who seems as if they might be her parents. Or friends. No one young, even, apart from me and the family in black. Most of the others might as well be random people off the street. I wonder, briefly, if the two women near me are social workers, or something like that.

As soon as the last prayer is over, I think, I'll leave the church.

The boy in the pew behind me watches me as I get up. He half smiles, as if he recognises me, too, from somewhere. He's holding one of the babies on his lap, and something about that touches my heart for a second.

It's a relief to get into fresh air, daylight. What did I think was going to happen? Some revelation, perhaps. Or a way to close the door on the incident that caught me up, involuntarily and at random. If anything is ever random, that is.

I walk back along the high street towards the station, past the café, past the run-down shops and market. Amidst all the normal busy city life, Bridie's death, her funeral and burial goes unnoticed and unmarked. The sky is tight stretched, a solid grey cloud above the streets and houses, but the air is sticky and warm. I take off the black jacket. I notice each tiny thing, and think: Bridie, whoever she was, will never see any of it, feel it, touch it, hear it or anything, ever again.

On the train back, I open my sketchbook and look again at the drawings I did in the café. An image of that family keeps coming to me: all ages, all talking and laughing and quarrelling and being a normal big family. And against that, thrown into stark relief, the solitary figure of the girl. Bridie.

Images of discord, I think. Just a project, for Art. That's all.

Mum's having a cup of tea at the kitchen table; she looks up from her magazine as I come in. 'Freya! Had a good day? You're later than usual.'

‘OK. Tiring.’ I pour myself an orange juice, take it out to the garden.

Mum follows, cup of tea in hand. She flops down in a deckchair. ‘It’s the weather, making you tired. The air pressure’s building up for a storm. See all the thunderflies?’

‘How was your day?’ I ask her.

‘Fine. Busy. I’m glad it’s Friday. Got any plans for the weekend?’

‘Miranda and me’ll go out tonight, I expect. I’ll phone her later.’

I don’t tell Mum where I’ve been. She’d be cross. Upset. I have to keep so many things from her these days and it makes us distant. I hate it but I don’t know what to do to change it. To get back to how we were before Joe died. I’m starting to realise how lonely it makes me feel.

I text Miranda. We arrange to meet at Back to Mine, at nine thirty. She’s hoping Charlie, from her Geography class, will be there. I don’t tell her why I wasn’t at English and she doesn’t ask.

Upstairs, I lie on my bed and stare out of the window at the top of the tree. Birds – swifts – fly high, swooping for flies, screaming their shrill high cries. I find an email from Danny, inviting me to London for a weekend.

Five

I'm just coming out of the studios the following Monday when I see the boy with the curly hair. I'm sure it's him. The one from the funeral, with his family. So that's why he looked familiar. I look again, to make sure. It's definitely him.

'Hi!' He nods at me as I go past.

Does he remember me, from the church?

At break, I go back to the studios to get my jacket and he's still there, working on some big colourful painting. His name's pinned on the board, marking out his studio space: *Gabriel Fielding.*

He sees me looking, and I blush, but neither of us says anything. I find my jacket on the back of a chair, and I walk out again. I'm meeting Miranda for coffee before we go to English together. He watches me go. I can feel his eyes on me.

After that, I keep seeing him – not just at college, but in town, too. We go to the same places, I guess. It's hardly surprising. It's not exactly a big city. I like the way he looks, and I like his artwork, too. But what am

I going to say if he asks me about why I was at that funeral? I'll just look weird.

'Who *is* that guy?' Miranda says. We're having lunch outside at the Boston café on Friday afternoon. 'He keeps looking at you.'

'He's one of the Art Foundation students,' I say. I don't look up.

Miranda smiles. 'And very good-looking. And clearly interested, Freya!'

'He's so not,' I say. 'He's never said more than hi to me.'

'That's a start,' Miranda says. 'Hi.'

I laugh. 'Not everyone's like you, so fixated on relationships. There's more to life than love and sex, you know.'

She laughs too. 'Is there? Really? Like what, for instance?'

'Friends. Finding out what you really want to do. Being creative. Having fun. Swimming. Saving the planet. Making a difference to the world. Want me to go on?'

'Not really. Anyway, you can do all that and be in love. Everyone needs love.'

'How's it going with Charlie?' I ask. 'Seeing as we're talking *love*.'

'OK. He invited me to watch him play at the Bell at the weekend.'

'That's progress.'

'Well, he asked lots of people. Not just me.'

'Ah.'

'Exactly.' Miranda sighs. 'I'm just one of the crowd.'

I glance over at Gabriel, sitting with a small group of other art students at one of the tables under a sun umbrella. White cotton shirt, sleeves rolled up. Jeans. Flip-flops. Nice. There are three girls in the group, but they all just seem like good friends. He's almost always in a group of people. I think again about that big family – his family, I presume. He's at ease with people.

'You could come,' Miranda says.

'Where?'

'To the pub, on Saturday night.'

'You have to be eighteen,' I say. 'They always check. You won't get in, either.'

Miranda checks her phone. 'I'm going to be late for Geography if I don't go now,' she says.

'I'll stay and finish my coffee,' I say. 'And see you later, yes?'

Miranda picks up her bag. She leans over and whispers in my ear. 'He's still there, and still looking. Play your cards right and you're in.'

'Stop it! Have fun in Geography. Say hello to Charlie from me.'

Two of the girls from the group at Gabriel's table get up to leave. They each hug Gabriel as they go past his chair. I get my notebook out, and start drawing. I try to draw the market stall opposite, and the Polish man selling strawberries. I'm still no good at doing people. I've got Life Drawing next term, so I need to get better. It's hard to get the proportions right, and my people look flat: surface decoration rather than three-dimensional figures. I draw the pigeons that are picking scraps out of the gutter near the corner shop. It's less busy now: end of lunch hour. People go back to their offices, college classes, wherever.

I'm conscious of a figure standing next to me. I look up, and it's him: Gabriel, carrying an empty glass.

'Want another coffee?' he says. 'I'm getting myself one.'

'Thanks!' I've gone hot. Bright red, probably. 'A cappuccino, please.'

He comes back with the two cups and he sits down at my table as if that's a perfectly natural thing to do. I glance over to where he was sitting before. The people he was with have all left.

I don't know why I've suddenly gone so self-conscious. It's like when I had that crush on Matt, years ago. Izzy's boyfriend. Maybe it's because Gabriel reminds me of him a bit: the fair hair, blue eyes. Confident.

'I'm Gabes,' he says.

'Freya.'

'You doing Art A level?'

I nod.

'It's a good course,' he says. 'I did it last year. Fun. Now I'm doing the Art Foundation.'

I sip my coffee.

'I've seen you somewhere else,' he says. 'Haven't I? In Exeter. A funeral. It was you, wasn't it?'

I nod.

'How come you knew Bridie?'

'I didn't.'

He frowns. 'I don't get it. What were you doing there, then?'

I take a deep breath. 'It's very complicated.'

He looks at me. 'So, tell me.'

'Something awful happened.'

I tell him about the train.

He listens. At one point he winces, though he doesn't interrupt. 'It must have been really shocking,' he says when I've finished. 'I can kind of understand why you wanted to find out who it was. It's like . . . seeing something through. Anyone would be a bit curious, wouldn't they?'

'Would they?' I'm not so sure. Most people would just want to forget the whole thing. It happens a lot, apparently. The train people try to cover up *how* often, exactly.

'And you? Did you . . . I mean, how did you know her?' I ask.

'That's a bit complicated too.' He stops talking, and for a moment I'm not sure what to do. Is he thinking? Deciding whether to tell me? But he starts up again.

'We knew her a long time ago. When she was little. So when she heard what had happened, Mum wanted us to go. She guessed there wouldn't be many people there. We all went, the whole family, except for my older brother.' He smiles at me. 'We must have looked pretty weird, all of us in that church in our smart clothes.'

'No. I thought – well, I think it's nice you did that for her. I wish I had a big family like yours.'

Already, I've said too much. He wants to know about

my family, and before long I'm telling him about Joe, and my whole life history, almost.

We've both finished our coffees. I look at my watch. We've been here over an hour. I've missed English.

'I'd better be going back,' I say.

'I'll walk with you.'

By the time we get into college the art studios are empty.

'What's your project, this term?' he asks.

'Discord.'

He laughs.

'Why's it funny?'

'I don't know. It's like, that's what adults think will *engage young people*, or something. That we're all into conflict, and dark stuff; graffiti, street art; rebellion. It makes me laugh. Some ancient examiners will have sat round a table and come up with it as the theme for the exam, and been all excited about what a good idea they've had.'

I frown. 'I hadn't thought of it like that. It's actually quite interesting. Gives us lots of scope. I think it's a good topic.'

'Sorry. Didn't mean to come over all cynical. I'm not, usually.'

'So, what's your work all about, then?'

'Colour. Colour and light.'

'Can I see?'

He shows me the huge abstract painting he's working on: luminous greens and yellows, with a splash of dark purple in one corner. Acrylics and oil paints. I leaf through his notebooks, full of pencil sketches of plants, and gardens, and then pastel colour sketches. I can see the way his abstract images emerge from the real-life drawings, so what you end up with is shape, and colour, and something more . . . His painting is full of joy.

'Where did you do the sketches?' I ask.

'Home, mostly: the garden, and the fields around where I live.'

'In the countryside?'

'Yes, though it's not that far from town, really.'

'It looks amazing.'

'It's not really. I mean, the garden's a kind of jungly mess. It's not like a perfect garden or anything. But it's a mass of colour in summer.'

'Sounds nice.'

'It is. You should come and see it some time.'

'I'd love to,' I say.

People are spilling out of hot classrooms into the corridor, suddenly. It's the end of the college day.

'I'm going home now,' I say.

'Me too. Want a lift?'

'You've got a car?'

He laughs. 'No. A scooter. Vintage Honda. Very slow, very old.' He picks up a shiny black helmet from under the table. 'So?'

'I'm fine walking, thanks!'

I look back, once, and he's still standing there, at the college entrance, the helmet dangling from his hand, watching me. I wave.

Miranda catches me up at the end of the road. 'What happened?'

'We had coffee. We talked. He showed me his studio space.'

She grins. 'Not bad. Worth missing English for?'

'Definitely. What did I miss, exactly?'

'New book: by George Eliot, who is a woman not a man. *The Mill on the Floss*. We're supposed to read as much of it as we can over the weekend. It's really old fashioned. Heavy going. But Nigel says it's worth it. Now, tell me more about Gabriel. When are you seeing him next?'

'I don't know. We didn't arrange anything *specific*.'

'Honestly, Freya! You are so totally hopeless! Did you swap mobile numbers?'

'No, course not.'

'I'll find out his for you. Charlie might know.'

'You just want an excuse to talk to Charlie.'

'Of course!'

We've got to the corner of my street. We both stop, hug.

'OK, see ya! Call me later, yes?' Miranda carries on up the main road.

I walk down our hill, not walking on the cracks between the paving stones, like we used to do, Joe and I, when we were little. Lines from a song flit into my head. Something Mum used to sing. Carly Simon? Joni Mitchell?

She'll be waiting for me, wanting to hear about my day. I prepare myself. I won't mention Gabes.

Six

Miranda would be proud of me. Yesterday at college Gabes asked me if I wanted to go and see his house and the garden in his paintings, and I said yes.

I check my watch. It's seven thirty already. People are heading down the street to the multiplex cinema. I walk along a bit, next to the wall, and lean against it under the tree.

I hear the *phut phut* sound of the bike engine before I see the bike. Only Gabes could make an old scooter bought off eBay look cool. But he does. Even in his funny old-style bike helmet. He's wearing the white shirt I like, skinny jeans and blue Converse.

He unbuckles the spare helmet for me. 'Been on the back of a bike before?'

'Never.'

'It's perfectly safe. I'll drive very slowly. Especially uphill.' He laughs. 'You'll have to hold on to me. And lean the same way as me and the bike, don't try to counterbalance.'

'How far is it?'

'Not very. Takes about twenty minutes.'

Gabes leans forward to help me fasten the strap. So close up, his breath is warm on my face. His skin smells slightly sweet, like soap. 'There!' he says. 'Ready?'

He gets on first, to balance the bike while I climb behind him. I put my hands lightly on his waist.

Everything about this first journey is exciting: him, the bike, the speed, compared to my old push-bike – and it gets more so as we climb out of the city and leave the main roads for small leafy lanes between high hedges. It's so green! A green wash of light through leaves, the lane making a tunnel under arching tall beech trees, and then the trees give way to open fields on either side, and down a steep valley, across a bridge over a stream, up the other side so slowly that I'm afraid the engine will give out altogether, though it doesn't. Next comes another long flat stretch through woods. I don't know this side of the city so well. I don't really know where I am, and then suddenly we're turning off the lane, down a steep, stony drive, into a cobbled yard and I see the house.

It's very old, built of stone, with small windows and a low, stone-tiled roof. It's like stepping back in time. Swallows swoop across the yard and up under the eaves of the roof, back and forth in criss-crossing lines.

Gabes turns off the engine and silence folds back in, except for the *tick tick* as it cools down. Gradually I hear other sounds, too: birdsong, and the hum of hundreds of bees on a tall bank of white and pink wildflowers. For a moment we just sit there, and then I take my hands off Gabes' waist, and climb down, and he parks the bike on its stand. I take off my helmet and fluff out my hair with my hands.

The door is open. I will discover, later, that it's almost always like this, unlocked. That Gabes' parents trust that things will be all right, that there's no need to worry about locks and property and possessions. We step over the threshold into a big kitchen, with a wooden table in the middle, a jumble of plates and mugs and books and piles of paper, and a china jug of the wildflowers I saw outside, spilling dusty yellow pollen over the wooden surface. The cushions on the chairs – all different, not matching – are faded as if they have been left out in the sun too long. I take it all in: the row of boots by the door; a big dresser with china plates and cups and saucers, bits and pieces from different sets, as if they've been picked up over many years from different places, or handed down through many generations. Tiled floor. Double stove, a row of wooden cupboards. A big bowl of ripe fruit – Victoria plums, from their own orchard, his mum tells me later, and another bowl, of their own eggs.

Gabes puts his bike helmet on the table on top of a pile of papers, flicks on the kettle, opens the fridge and peers inside. 'Hungry? Want a sandwich? Supper won't be for ages.'

I shake my head. 'No thanks.' I pull out a chair and sit down.

Gabes butters bread, cuts a thick slab of cheese, piles on pickle and tomatoes, takes big, hungry bites. 'How was your first ride, then?'

'Exciting!'

'Good,' he says through a mouthful. 'We almost didn't make it. Hardly any petrol. I only realised that halfway back. But I didn't tell you, in case you got worried.'

I think of my journey home, later, but I don't say anything. Instead, I ask, 'Where is everyone? Are they expecting me?'

'Of course!' he says through another huge mouthful. 'They're around somewhere, I expect.'

In this house, visitors are obviously no big deal. If this were my home, Mum would be hovering, waiting to say hello the minute we arrived, wanting to be hospitable, but never really relaxed: offering drinks and food and not knowing what to say, and ending up just being in the way. She doesn't realise what she's like.

'I'll show you round, in a bit,' Gabes says. 'If you want.'

I do.

'How old is it?'

'The house? Pre-Domesday.'

'Really? Which means what, exactly?'

'Eleventh century, in the very oldest part. Other bits were added on: each generation added more. The Domesday book was 1080-something. You know, when they made a census of all the people and houses in Britain.'

I try to imagine what it would be like to live somewhere so extraordinarily ancient. Do houses have memories? I used to think so, that places hold an imprint of the things that happen in them, of life and death and love and all the things between.

'How long have you lived here?' I ask.

'My whole life. I was born here. Literally. Upstairs, in the little back bedroom. Same for Theo, and Kit, and Laura and Beth.'

'Your brothers and sisters?'

'Yes.'

'So, who's who?'

'Theo's twenty-one. He's at university. Kit's sixteen. Beth's married to Will and they have twin babies, Phoebe and Erin. They live in Oxford, though lately Beth's been staying here a lot. Laura lives in London with her boyfriend, so they just visit. Most weekends, in fact. Laura doesn't like London much.'

I'm suddenly really jealous. Why couldn't I have a proper big family like this?

'What do your mum and dad do?' I ask.

'Dad's a vet. Mum writes books.'

I look up as the door opens, and a woman comes into the kitchen as if on cue. 'Who writes books?' she asks.

'You do,' Gabes says. 'Remember?'

Her hair's wet, as if she's just stepped out of the shower. She's wrapped in a blue cotton dressing gown, so loosely done up that when she sits down at the table opposite me it flaps open and I have to try not to notice how naked she is underneath.

'Hello, Freya,' she says. 'I'm Maddie. Gabes' mum.'

I'm suddenly shy. She doesn't seem to notice. 'I hope he drove very carefully and slowly,' she says.

'He did.'

'Good. That's the one advantage of having such an old bike,' she says.

Gabes pulls a face.

'I'll get dressed in a minute,' she says. 'I had a bath and then I nearly fell asleep, reading on the bed. I'll start supper soon. You two could go and pick some beans for me. Has he shown you the garden, Freya?'

I shake my head. 'Not yet.'

'It's Mum's pride and joy,' Gabes explains.

'Nick's not back yet,' Maddie says. 'We'll wait for him before we eat. Laura and Tom are around, I think, and Beth's staying. She's doing the babies right now.' She smiles. 'Sorry, Freya. Too many names!'

'No,' I say. 'I like it – I mean – that there are so many of you –' My voice fades out. It doesn't sound quite the right thing to say.

The vegetable garden is round the back of the house – or is it the front? We came in the back, where the yard and the kitchen door are, but the real front of the house with a porch and big wooden door is the other side. The sun has dipped lower in the sky and the light is golden, spreading huge shadows. The swallows are flying low, swooping over the house and garden for flies.

We walk along a grassy path past a bed of herbs, tall spikes of fennel and late-flowering lavender, to the wigwam of beans. We start to pick the long green pods. Gabes' hand touches mine as we reach for the same pod and my heart skips a beat. The evening sun filters through green leaves. The grasses rustle; fine clouds of seeds blow across the garden. A petal falls from a wild red poppy. Music drifts from an open upstairs window.

Even as it happens, I'm thinking about it, aware of it happening. I'm falling in love: with a place, and a family, and a boy with curly hair and blue eyes.

Why do we say *falling* in love?

Like *falling* asleep.

The suddenness? The lack of control?

Seven

Halfway through the meal and I'm drunk with happiness. Not with alcohol, though that is flowing freely enough among the adults: Nick and Maddie, at opposite ends of the big oak table, are passing a bottle of red wine between them, via Beth, and Laura and her boyfriend, Tom, who are sitting along one side of the table, opposite me, Gabes and Kit. Nick's only just come from work at a farm three miles away: a sick cow. When Gabes mentioned 'vet' I'd thought of a town practice: cats and dogs and guinea pigs, but I've learned already that most of Nick's work is on farms. The roast lamb is a present from a satisfied customer. We're having it with the beans we picked, home-grown potatoes and mint and Maddie's home-made redcurrant sauce.

About three conversations are happening at the same time, one about books, one about cows, and the other about babies, as far as I can tell because I'm hardly following any of them, just lapping up the warm feeling of being included in this relaxed, open family, and feeling sleepy, now, because it's already late, and I've eaten too much.

Maddie pushes back her chair. She wipes her hair from her face with the back of one hand. Her hair has dried to a dark, wavy mass over her shoulders. She's changed into a white embroidered top and linen trousers. She looks far too young to have two such grown-up daughters. Nick's a lot older than her, his messy dark hair streaked with grey. He's tall, solid; comfortable-looking in a soft blue cotton shirt and faded jeans.

'Pudding, everyone?' Maddie says. She starts clearing the plates, and Laura and Tom get up to help.

I feel I should do something too. I look at Maddie and she smiles back. 'Would you get the cream from the fridge, Freya? Thanks.'

I help carry the dirty plates and serving bowls over to the sink. I open the fridge to find the cream.

'Plum crumble, with Victoria plums from our orchard,' Maddie announces as she puts the big bowl in the middle of the table. 'And fresh raspberries. You might need to pick them over. The late-fruiting ones get little worms inside, sometimes.'

'Extra protein,' Nick says. 'All the worms eat is raspberry, so it doesn't matter if you eat them.'

Gabes laughs. He's seen my face. 'Just have the plum crumble, Freya, then you'll be safe.'

'How's the book coming on, Maddie?' Laura asks.

'Slowly. Just started chapter six.' She sighs. 'There's never enough time. I should be sitting down to it every morning, soon as you lot have gone off.'

'You should stop doing the garden,' Beth says. 'Think of all the extra hours that would give you for writing.'

'The garden is my lifeline,' Maddie says. 'It's the one thing I do that keeps me sane. And anyway, what would we eat?'

'Food from supermarkets, like normal people,' Kit says. 'Can I go, now? I don't want pudding.'

'At this hour? Where?'

'A party,' Kit says.

'And how are you proposing to get there? And back?'

'I've got a lift, if I go now. Alex's mum.' He leaves the table, and no one stops him.

Maddie and Beth are already deep in a discussion about some children's book about an elephant and a baby. I half listen. A wail starts up from upstairs, and Beth gets up to go and sort out the crying child, and Laura and Tom get up to make coffee and little by little the table empties, as people take drinks and coffees into the sitting room, until finally just Gabes and I are left.

'Well,' he says, when he's finished stacking plates and bowls and cups into the dishwasher. 'You've met almost everyone, now. The big happy family.'

'I loved it,' I say. 'Thank you.'

Gabes rinses the pans and leaves them to drain. I watch him moving around the kitchen, methodically clearing up. He does it as if it's a perfectly normal thing for him to do.

'What time do you have to get home?' he says as he dries his hands.

'Eleven, at the latest. How shall I get back though?'

'I'll take you.'

'I thought you'd run out of petrol?'

'Dad'll have some, in the garage.' He comes over and stands behind my chair. He rests his hands for a second on the chair back, right up close to my shoulders.

I shiver.

'Come and see the rest of the house, first,' Gabes says.

He takes my hand, and I follow him, heart thumping, trying to take in the stone-flagged floor and the oak staircase and the creaky wooden boards on the landing that he presents me with, as if he is giving me a guided tour at a stately home. We pass three closed bedroom doors, and then go down one step.

'Mind your head,' he says, ducking under a beam and through a low doorway. 'People used to be smaller, in olden times.'

But I don't need to duck.

'And this is my room.'

It's small with white walls. A square window with a deep stone sill is set into the wall under the roof at one end. There's a single bed with a red cover, and a red and gold wool rug on the floor, bookshelves and a dark wooden desk and chair. A tabby cat curled at the foot of the bed lifts its head and stares, blinking, as Gabes switches on the light.

The cat purrs as I smooth her head. She pushes her paws at the bedcover, flexing her claws. Gabes leans over and strokes along her spine, and the cat turns to let him stroke her belly.

He lies back against the pillow and watches me. I'm still sitting at the foot of the bed, with the cat.

'You could stay over, if you wanted,' he says. 'There's plenty of spare beds. Then tomorrow I could show you the other cool places round here. The orchard, and the stream. There's a place we go swimming.'

I flush. 'No, I said I'd be back. My parents . . .'

'Another time, then. Come for the whole weekend.'

I hear voices, laughter, as people come upstairs – Laura and Tom, I think. No one seems bothered that I'm here. I'm just accepted: Gabes' friend Freya.

'What sort of books does your mother write?' I ask him.

'Novels. Short stories.' He stretches across to the bookshelves and pulls out a book with a dark green cover and the title *What We Love* in white lettering, and her name: *Madeleine Fielding*.

'What's it about?'

'No idea. Haven't read it.' He laughs.

All the way home on the bike, I sit pressed close to his back, my arms tight round his waist. It's much colder now that it is dark, and damp under the trees. The sound of the stream is louder than I remember on the way here. The beam of the headlight seems to fade into the dark too quickly. We don't pass a single car until we get to the first main road, and then there are orange streetlights, and people staggering home, and it's a different kind of journey altogether.

He drops me at the top of my road, in case my parents are looking out of the window: there's no way I'm letting them see me on the back of the bike!

'I'll see you Monday, then.'

'Yes. Thanks for the lift, and everything.' I hand him back the helmet and he straps it behind his seat.

'We could go for coffee,' he says. 'After college next week.'

'Yes. Great.'

I almost run down the hill, my heart singing. This is the beginning of my new life at last.

Eight

'Freya?' Mum calls down the stairs, the minute I get into the hall. 'Everything OK?'

'Yes. All good,' I call back. I wait for her to get into bed again, before I go through to the kitchen and sit down. I don't want to have to talk to anyone. I want to savour my whole evening.

Our kitchen looks stark, overly neat and clean and organised, compared to where I've just come from. Dad being an architect, he's got strong views on how things should look. He likes functional, clean design: straight lines, no clutter. Since Joe's death, Mum seems to spend many more hours each day cleaning and tidying and sorting, to stop her sitting and thinking too much. Being active keeps the feelings at bay, she says. It's what swimming does for me. I swim every day during the summer holidays when I'm on St Ailla.

My clothes are still damp from the ride home. My reflection in the kitchen window shows messy hair curling round my face and over my shoulders, and I smile. I don't belong in this too neat, too perfect house.

I'm a changeling child, and my real family are somewhere else . . .

A quick rush of guilt comes over me. I stand at the window, staring into the blank darkness outside. I think of the train accident girl, *Bridie.* I meant to ask Gabes more about her, and I completely forgot. Next time. I fill a glass with cold water from the jug in the fridge, and sip at it as I go upstairs to bed. I lie on my back for ages, my head whirling.

When I close my eyes, I can see green leaves, and golden evening sunlight, and the swoop and curve of swallows, diving for flies.

'Phone, Freya!' Mum's yelling up the stairs.

I've only just woken up. I can hear her talking to whoever it is, while she waits for me to come down. Someone she knows. Or she's being embarrassingly chatty to one of my friends. But who would use the house phone?

'Danny,' she says, when I reach the bottom stair. She passes me the phone.

'Hi, Danny,' I say, cautiously.

'You haven't been answering texts or emails.' Danny launches straight in. 'So I thought I'd phone your house. About you maybe coming up to London next weekend?' His voice goes up at the end, like a question.

'It's nine thirty on a Sunday morning, Danny!'

'Is it? Sorry. Did I wake you?'

'Never mind that now.' I sigh. 'The thing is, Danny, I've got way too much college work at the moment. I've got a huge Art project, and coursework for Biology and

English . . .' *And there's Gabes* . . . But I don't say that to Danny.

The first summer I went back to St Ailla after Joe died, Danny was amazing. Bit by bit, I told him everything. He was the first person who really listened to what it was like for me, losing Joe. It was Danny's first visit to the island: I showed him round; shared all the special places with him. I taught him how to snorkel; introduced him to all my other friends. We stayed in touch between summers: emails, the odd phone call, but that's all. And then this summer, the weather messed up everything.

The things we do together are all connected with being on the island: swimming and snorkelling; evening games of football on the field above Periglis with everyone from the campsite . . . parties on the beach round a fire . . . It's hard to imagine what it would be like to see him in London.

'You've gone very quiet,' Danny says.

'Sorry. I was thinking.'

'And?'

'Maybe I could come to London later on, when I haven't got so much work. You must have loads too. The Christmas holidays, perhaps?'

Danny sighs.

'Danny?'

'It doesn't matter,' Danny says. 'I guess you're too busy with all your new college friends, now.' He sounds hurt. 'So I'll see you some time. Around. Whatever.' And before I can say anything he puts the phone down on me.

Mum's hovering. Because of the open-plan layout, there's no privacy downstairs. 'Such a lovely boy!' she says. 'I know Evie's very fond of him. Are you going to meet up with him?'

'No.' I *so* do not want to talk about Danny with Mum. I go over to the window and stare at the sunny garden with my back to her.

She takes the hint. 'I've made coffee, if you want some. And how about an egg? Toast?'

'Just coffee. I'm still full from last night.'

'Did you have a good time?'

'Yes.'

'You were very late back.'

'Mum!'

'I know, but you're only sixteen, still.'

'It was Saturday night!'

'So, what are your plans for today?'

'I've got college work, then I'm meeting Miranda.'

We take our coffees out into the garden. Dad's away, on a work thing, so it's just the two of us. Mum talks on and on about what she's planning to plant next, and I drift off, not really listening, because there's nothing I can say but yes, and good, and well done, Mum. But I'm glad it makes her happy. I peel back my top, to let the sun get to my shoulders.

Miranda's waiting for me at the bridge over the river, at the start of the track leading up to the canal. I'm already sweaty from cycling from our house; she looks perfectly cool and collected.

'How was it? Your evening with Gabes.' She hugs me.

'Amazing!'

'Tell me everything!'

We cycle single file up the footpath to keep clear of the overgrown stinging nettles either side, but once we're up on the flat towpath there's room for us to cycle side by side and it's easier to talk.

'He lives in this ancient house, in the middle of the countryside. He's got a huge family, and his mum and dad are really cool and relaxed about everything. We all had supper together.'

Miranda pulls a face. 'It doesn't sound much like a proper date, though. I mean, a family meal! Freya! Why didn't you two go off somewhere, together?'

'It was fine. Honestly. I wanted to meet them all, that was the whole point, because we'd been talking about families. That's all. It's no big deal, Miranda.' I swerve to avoid an overhanging bramble. A baby rabbit shoots back from the grassy verge into the undergrowth. All summer you see them, nibbling at the grass beside the towpath, and as the summer wears on they get fewer and fewer, as they meet their untimely deaths: foxes, or bikes . . .

It's Miranda's turn to talk: Charlie's amazing saxophone playing, and how she wants to go with him and a load of others to Glastonbury, next summer. *You've got to come too, Freya! Pleease?* We get to the gate where we turn off down to the level crossing, and we lock up the bikes while a high-speed train from London thunders past. I think of Bridie. It's as if she's permanently etched on my mind, now. But I don't say anything to Miranda this time.

We spread my rug out on the grass near the river, so we can see the weir and watch people. It's not as hot as it has been; we talk, and read a bit, and then I get up to go for a swim.

'Please come!' I say to Miranda. 'It's more fun with you.'

She shivers. 'It's too cold. And I don't like the mud, and not being able to see what's underneath. But I'll watch you from here.'

Under the willow trees, the light falls in triangles of golden sunlight. I swim slowly upstream, long leisurely strokes, holding my breath as my face goes under, taking steady breaths as I turn my head before dipping in for the next stroke. The rhythm is deeply restful, the water flows like silk over my body. Hardly anyone else swims this far from the weir; most come to play, and hang out, rather than for serious swimming. And that's not why I do it, either. But the feel of moving on, through water, is something my body needs, and it's the only way, sometimes, that I can calm down the wild turmoil in my mind, when thoughts go on overdrive.

I've gone beyond the stretch of the river where Miranda will be able to see me, should she actually be looking. Which is unlikely. She's probably reading.

I wonder about the stream near his house where Gabes said you can swim. I can't imagine it being deep or wide enough just there, but perhaps I'm wrong. How will it be, when I see him on Monday at college?

A bird skims low in front of me: so close I see the moment when it scoops up a beakful of fly and river water. A swallow, again. They are everywhere this summer. Danny's hurt voice briefly flits into my mind, and I put it out again, quickly.

I lie on my back to float, though it's hard work to keep still, with the river current pulling me downstream. An image comes: that Pre-Raphaelite painting by Millais, of Ophelia, drowned in the river with flowers in her hair. Ophelia from *Hamlet*. And I remember reading something about the woman who was the artist's model; Lizzie someone. She caught cold from lying in the bath water too long, didn't she?

When I finally emerge from the river, dripping and shivery, the field is full of shadow. The sun is covered by a fine skein of cloud, mottled like the back of a mackerel. The weather's changing. It already smells different.

Miranda's hands me a towel. 'Hurry up! You were ages. It's gone all cold and horrible. I want to go back.'

We cycle back fast along the towpath. The air smells of wood smoke; several of the narrowboats have lit their stoves already. It begins to spit with rain. Summer is over.

Nine

Gabes and I have coffee together most days the next week. We just chat, it's very relaxed and casual. We don't touch, or anything physical at all. Perhaps he just sees me as another ordinary friend, like all his others. I'm slightly disappointed, but I don't let on, even to Miranda. Then, on Friday, he invites me to spend Saturday at his house and I say yes. Same arrangements as before: he'll pick me up from the road near college, on his bike, but in the morning this time. Eleven.

So here I am. This time I'm more prepared for the ride: sensible clothes, a waterproof jacket, gloves. It's beginning to rain.

'Hi, Freya!' Gabes is right on time. He hands me the spare helmet and waits for me to climb on behind him. We set off down the street, turn off for the roundabout and chug slowly up the hill. It's not nearly so much fun in the rain. I pull the visor down to cover my face. Lorries sail past us, splashing water up over my legs. It's a relief when we turn off the main road on to the quiet lane.

I'm leaning into his back, arms tight round his waist and my head down because of the wind and the wet, so I don't see the bend in the lane coming up. The bike seems to tip: my instinct is to lean the other way, to balance.

My big, stupid mistake.

Everything happens so fast I hardly know what is happening. The bike skids on the wet tarmac, I spill off the back, the bike goes over into the bank. I can hear the *tick tick* of the dying engine. There's no sign of Gabes.

There's one of those weird, slow-motion, silent moments that happens after accidents – as if you've fallen into something, the pause between one note and the next – before the usual sounds of everyday life fold back again: the *cheep cheep* of a bird in the hedge, rain dripping on to leaves, wind rippling the long grass along the verge.

I'm not hurt. I sit up, stretch each limb to make quite sure, but I'm fine.

I stand up. I'm covered in mud and grass seeds. I adjust the helmet, which must have slipped sideways as I hit the ground. It did its job, though. Saved my head. 'Gabes?' I call. 'You all right?'

There's a sort of grunting noise. I walk further up the lane. I can see him now, sticking half out of the ditch next to the hedge. I start to laugh. 'I'm so sorry,' I say. 'I leant the wrong way. I know you said not to but I forgot. It was all my fault.'

He shifts position. He grimaces as he moves. 'I've done something to my foot. Broken it or sprained badly. It hurts.'

I stop laughing, though he still looks funny, sitting in a ditch. 'What can I do? Shall I help you get up?'

I pull and he heaves himself up, and we get him out of the muddy water on to the grass, and then he lies back, white-faced.

'Got your phone?'

I nod.

'Better call home. Mum'll come out and get us.'

I hand him my phone while I go to pick up the bike and push it towards the verge, out of the road. It's heavy. Luckily the lane's deserted. We skidded right across, and if something had been coming the other way, fast . . . Better not to think like that.

We settle back down on the wet grass to wait. I can tell he's in pain, but he doesn't grumble much. He's annoyed about the bike, and about being stuck, and now a broken – we're sure it *is* broken – foot. 'I'll be stuck at home, at the mercy of my parents giving me lifts,' he says.

A car comes along the lane. The driver slows down when he sees us, winds down his window. 'You two OK? Need a ride somewhere?'

I shake my head. 'No thanks. We're all sorted.'

It's only about ten more minutes before we hear another car, and Maddie appears, driving their green van.

'You poor loves!' she says, getting out. 'Oh, Gabes! Your foot! It's all twisted. You look awful!'

Between us, his arms round our shoulders, we manage to help him to the van door and up into the front seat. Then we push the bike over and lift that up between us, into the back.

'Hop in next to Gabes,' Maddie says to me. 'We'll go via Home Farm and then you can wait there while I take Gabes to Accident and Emergency. Are you sure you're not hurt at all, Freya? It must have been quite a shock.'

I nod. 'I'm fine. Really.'

'Nick could have a quick look at Gabes' foot, first, I guess,' Maddie says. 'We don't want to end up at the hospital unless it's strictly necessary.'

'I thought Nick was a vet?' I say.

'He is. But it's much the same: animals, people, broken bones.'

That makes me laugh.

Maddie switches the radio on. The rain sweeps over the big front windscreen. It's nice being higher up, in the van. You can see over the tops of the hedges. Well, you could, if it wasn't so rainy and misty. It's cosy, the three of us bowling along together. I almost wish we were going on a proper journey. A holiday or something.

'How did it happen, exactly?' Maddie asks. 'Tell me properly.'

Kind, generous Gabes says he doesn't know, that it was just a skid on the wet road. He doesn't mention me leaning the wrong way, upsetting the balance. Doesn't blame me at all.

'Will the bike be all right?' I say.

'Probably,' Gabes says. He frowns again. His face has gone white, with two red splotches on his cheeks. He's obviously in pain.

The day we planned together is ruined, now. But at least Maddie hasn't suggested taking me straight back home.

The rain has stopped by the time we arrive at their house. Maddie parks the van in the courtyard.

'You stay here,' she says to Gabe. 'I'll go in quickly to see if Nick's around. You come with me, Freya.'

So I follow her into the house, and she fills the kettle and gets a flask out of a cupboard. 'The wait's bound to be horrendous. Better to be properly prepared.' She goes upstairs, calling for Nick.

I sit down at the table. I leaf through the pages of the colour magazine from the newspaper. The cat comes and sits on my lap.

Maddie hurries back into the kitchen with a book in one hand and Gabes' jumper and notebook in the other. 'Nick isn't here. No one is. So, just make yourself at home,' she says to me. 'Unless you want to come up to the hospital too, with Gabes? But it's probably better for you to stay here.'

'I'm fine here, as long as you don't mind,' I say.

'Beth and the twins won't be back till about four. I hope to be back long before that. But you'll tell them what happened, if necessary, won't you?'

'Of course.'

'Just help yourself to anything you need. Food, books, films, musical instruments, garden.' She sweeps her hand round. 'You'll find something to keep you happy, I'm sure.'

I wave from the door at Gabes as they go off. I walk

slowly back inside the house. I fill up the kettle again, to make tea. I chose myself a china mug from the row on hooks on the wooden dresser. I imagine what it would be like, to live here all the time.

At first it's a bit odd, being alone in someone else's house. I'm a bit nervous, expecting someone to walk through the door at any moment. After a while I relax. I go round the house, peering at pictures and photographs hanging on the walls, looking at the rows of bookshelves, taking it all in. Everything's old, and used, and nothing matches, and yet it all blends perfectly together. It looks random, but how can it be? I think about how in our house my dad has chosen everything really carefully, and with a particular colour or design in mind: Danish chairs, for their clean lines, and pale wood furniture, neutral colours. Miranda loves it. To her it's really cool and awesome.

Along the top of the piano are rows of photographs in frames: old ones, black-and-white, and a whole series of children at different ages and stages. I peer at the children's faces, trying to work out who is who. I think I can tell Gabes in most of them. And there's another boy, thinner and darker than Gabes, who must be Theo, the older brother at university. I lift up the lid of the piano and run my fingers over the keys, lightly to begin with, because the sound is almost shocking in such a silent house, and then I get more confident and I play the two pieces I know off by heart, from when I was little and had lessons. I go upstairs to the bathroom, and imagine lying in the big old bath, with a view out of the window to the orchard, in sunshine. There's a shelf of books in here, even, and a big framed oil painting of four children, from olden times. Perhaps they're Gabes' ancestors, who once lived in this house.

I pad along the landing and down the step to Gabes' room. His bed's unmade. I leaf through the pile of drawings on his table, and then feel guilty, as if I'm reading a private diary or something personal like that, even though the drawings are of the garden, mostly. It gives me the idea, though, of going outside, doing my own work while I wait. I borrow some paper and a bunch of pencils from Gabes' desk, and go back downstairs.

Everything's shiny in sunshine after rain. I go the way we went before, across the yard and round to the vegetable garden, and then through the gap in the wall to the orchard. The apple trees are weighed down with fruit, and wasps feed off the fallen plums in the grass. Hens scratch at the grass with their scaly feet, clucking and crooning at each other. They take no notice of me, as if they know I offer nothing. I find a dryish patch of stone to sit on, and I start to draw.

I'm not sure how long I've been there when I hear a car, and doors slamming, voices and a baby crying. I sit back, my drawing on my knees, to see what happens next. I'm hoping Beth will remember me; I didn't meet the children before. But it's not even nearly four o'clock. So perhaps it isn't her after all.

I screw up my eyes, because the sun's so bright. Someone is standing in the archway into the orchard:

a figure in silhouette, backlit. They come slowly across the damp grass, and I see a young man, a boy, really, with dark hair, and black jeans, and a black jacket. I recognise him instantly. Theo.

He doesn't smile.

I get up, ready to explain, to introduce myself, but before I can he's turned round and walked back through the arch.

I make my own way back to the kitchen, just in time to hear Theo say, 'There's a strange girl in the orchard.'

By the time I get to the door, he's disappeared inside, and Beth's there, one child on her hip, smiling at me. 'Hi, Freya!'

The little girl squirms to get down. She's only a toddler, with a fluff of fair hair, in a white cotton frock.

'Hello!' I say shyly. I start to explain. 'Maddie had to take Gabriel to the hospital –'

'I know, she phoned me; she said you'd be here. She's waiting while they X-ray his foot. Then she'll bring him home, once he's had his foot plastered or whatever they're going to do. I'm just about to make some lunch. Want some?'

'I can help if you like,' I say.

'Would you keep an eye on the girls?' Beth says. 'This is Phoebe. Erin's still sleeping in the car.'

I'm not really used to babies, but I do my best.

Phoebe solemnly hands me a book, and she lets me read it to her, though she won't sit on my lap to begin with. We sit side by side on the floor instead.

'Poor old Gabes,' Beth says, running lettuce under the tap. 'He'll hate being cooped up with a broken foot.'

She picks ripe tomatoes out of a bowl on the table and starts to slice them. 'What happened, exactly?'

I tell her. Phoebe tugs my hand, to make me read the book again. It's the one with the elephant and the baby that they were arguing about when I came to supper.

Beth clears some of the stuff off the table, and lays down the bowl of salad and plates and a wooden board with different cheeses. She fills a small green bowl with olives, and makes a dressing with limes and garlic. Even the smallest actions she makes somehow stylish. She licks olive oil off her fingers. 'So, you know Gabes from college, yes? Are you doing the same course?'

I shake my head. 'Just A levels, at the moment. I might do the Art Foundation afterwards, though. I haven't decided. What about you? What do you do?'

'I'm a mother. That's all I do these days.'

I flush. 'Well, that's a very good and important thing to do.'

She looks at me. 'Is it? Not many people seem to think so.'

I'm out of my depth, now; embarrassed. Luckily Phoebe's tugging at me again. I follow her into the front room, where she shows me a box of toys, and we start building things with coloured bricks. I make a house, and she knocks it down. That's her favourite thing, I work out: knocking things down.

Footsteps come down the stairs, and the dark shadow of the boy I saw before is there, suddenly, watching us.

'Hello,' I say. 'I'm Freya. Gabriel's friend.'

He nods, and goes on round to the kitchen.

I hear him, chatting to Beth in the kitchen, and then to Erin, who has woken up from her nap.

Lunch is chaotic with two small children, and no one seems to sit down at the same time throughout the whole meal, but I still love being there, part of it all. Theo doesn't say anything to me, but he's lovely with Erin, in particular. He lets her feed him bits of salad with a spoon. Most of it spills on to the table. We're just starting to clear the dishes when we hear the van. I go out into the yard just as Maddie's helping Gabes out of the front seat on to brand-new crutches.

'Are you OK? Is it broken?' I hover next to Gabes, wanting to help.

'Yep.' He holds out his foot, solid in bright blue plaster.

'I'm so, so sorry, Gabes!'

He hobbles and hops across the yard into the kitchen and collapses into the nearest chair. The crutches clatter to the floor. I pick them up, lean them against the table.

'We were quicker than I expected,' Maddie says. 'Best to break bones in the morning, I guess, rather than the evening with all the drunks and fights. There was hardly a queue.'

'Lunch, baby brother?' Beth asks Gabes. She starts heaping salad on to a plate for him, cuts a hunk of bread, butters it generously, as if he is a child.

I sit with him at the table while he eats, and then we go to the sitting room, so he can rest his leg up properly on cushions on the sofa.

'Does it hurt?' I run my finger gently down the plaster.

'A bit. They gave me strong painkillers.'

'I feel awful. It's all my fault.'

'Rubbish,' Gabes says. 'Stop saying that. It was an accident. The wet road.'

The cat pads into the room, jumps up on to Gabes' lap and starts paddling with her paws, settling down and purring loudly. I watch his hand, absent-mindedly smoothing her fur.

'Dad thinks the cat's pregnant,' Gabes says after a while. 'It's too early to tell for certain, but Dad has an instinct about these things and he's probably right.'

'I'm surprised you don't have a dog, living out here, with your huge garden and everything.'

'We did. She died, beginning of May. Mum wept for a week. It was awful.'

'I used to want a dog so much. A border collie. There were puppies at the farm on the island one summer.' I start to tell Gabes about St Ailla, but he's yawning, not really listening.

'Sorry,' he says. 'It's the painkillers. Making me sleepy.'

Maddie puts her head round the door to check on Gabes. 'Everything all right?' She laughs as he yawns noisily again, head back, mouth wide open. 'Perhaps you'd like me to take you home, Freya? He's not going to be very good company, by the look of it!'

A shadow comes in the doorway. Theo. 'I'm going for a swim,' he says quietly. 'She could come with me.'

'*She*? You mean Freya? It's not much of an invitation, put like that!' Maddie laughs again.

Theo makes a big drama out of rolling his eyes behind her back. 'It's turned out such a beautiful sunny afternoon, Freya. Would you care to join me for a swim in the river?' He puts on a mock posh accent. 'We can lend you a delightful bathing suit.' He looks at Maddie. 'Can we? Yours or Beth's? Would they fit?'

'I've got my own, thanks,' I say. 'In my bag. Just in case. Gabes said we might swim.'

We all look at Gabes, slumped down on the sofa now, already asleep.

'He won't be swimming for a while,' Maddie says. 'Poor old Gabriel. Up to you, Freya. It'll be cold, mind.'

'Not as cold as the sea, at my island,' I tell her. 'And I've been swimming there all summer, even in the rain.'

Theo is taller than Gabes, with much darker hair, and paler skin. He's dressed all in black. I still haven't seen him smile. But he's Gabes' brother, isn't he? So he must be OK, deep down. I know he's studying English at Oxford, so presumably he's clever, too, though I can't really tell, yet.

'How far is it?' I ask, as I gather up my things.

'Fifteen minutes' walk, max.' He leads the way across the yard, back up the rough track to the lane, then turns off almost immediately over a stile and down a footpath lined either side with stinging nettles, waist high, wet and droopy after the morning's rain. It smells damp and fresh.

The footpath goes downhill along the edge of a field.

I catch glimpses of the stream through gaps in the trees that line the banks, dappled silver. At the bottom of the field we climb another stile, on to the grassy path that runs along the stream bank. The water runs shallow over pebbles at this point, nowhere deep enough to swim, but further along the stream curves round and the pebbles give way to sandy mud and the water has scoured a series of deep pools.

Theo starts chanting poetry as he strides ahead. '"*Clear and cool, clear and cool, by laughing shallow and dreaming pool*" . . . Charles Kingsley, from *The Water Babies*,' he says, showing off. He stops at a patch of grass, and starts stripping off down to his boxers, surprisingly unself-conscious.

I can't help noticing how fit he is: his upper body and arms. I didn't expect that. Under all those baggy black clothes I never imagined he'd have the body of a dancer. Or a swimmer. I watch him dive cleanly into the top pool. As he surfaces, he shakes water off his hair like a wet otter.

'Come on, then!' He smiles at me for the first time.

'I need to change first!' I wish I'd thought to put on my swimsuit up at the house. Now I have to do it wriggling under my towel, crouched under a bit of hedge that turns out to have prickles on the branches. I know he's watching. I pull the black straps up over my shoulders and stand up. It's my proper swimsuit, not a skimpy bikini, but flattering, sophisticated in simple black.

'Where did you get a tan like that?' he calls from the stream.

'St Ailla,' I say. 'My island for the whole summer. Not that there was much sun.' I put my clothes together in a neat pile next to his. I dive in, making barely a splash. I can see he's impressed. He has no idea about me. It gives me huge pleasure to surprise him. I swim downstream, wading between the pools. The water is much clearer than the river at the weir. I swim with the current in the next stretch of the river, and when it finally gets too shallow, I wade to the bank and walk back up the path.

Theo's lying on his towel on the grass, sunning himself. He studies me for a minute, as if he's thinking what to say. 'So, you are a real water baby.'

'That's what my mother used to call me.' I feel myself flush. I pick up my towel to wipe my face, and to hide behind. My heart's pounding and I'm slightly out of breath after my long swim and the walk back. I dry myself and then spread out the towel next to Theo, and sit down. My skin tingles as it begins to warm up. I turn to face him. 'Swimming is what I love best.'

Theo studies me for a moment. 'Best out of what? You can't have *best*, without something to compare it with.'

'How *pedantic* you are,' I say. 'OK. Swimming is what I love.'

'Why not, *I love swimming*? Much more straightforward.'

I think about it. 'But it means something *subtly* different.' I smile. 'Surely you can see that? If you care about words, and language, so much.'

'Who says I do?'

'It's obvious. Because you're so picky about them. You are studying English, after all.'

'Reading. I'm *reading* English. That's what you are supposed to say.'

I laugh outright. 'You are pompous and ridiculous, Theo!'

He frowns.

You'd think in a big family he'd be used to being teased. But he's clearly annoyed.

We lie side by side in the afternoon sun without talking. Flies buzz in clouds above our heads, noisy and irritating. The undergrowth smells slightly rank as it steams gently in the warmth. It's a different sort of heat now it's autumn.

I notice a scar on the inside of Theo's arm, deep like a knife cut, but from long ago, healed to a silver line. There's something dark and unfathomable about this boy. He's very different from Gabes, or Beth, or Kit, even, for that matter. For a fleeting moment I think of that girl again: Bridie. I haven't asked Gabes about her yet. I daren't ask Theo.

Theo props himself up on his elbows, leaning backwards. 'We've swum here since we were small children. Maddie used to bring us,' he says. 'But Gabes is never that keen. I'm surprised he asked you over for a swim. I wonder why?'

'Because he knows it's what I love?' I say. I know he's implying something else, something more cynical, but I won't take the bait.

'And I get the privilege instead. Poor old Gabes!'

I get up. 'I'm going to change.' I take my clothes and

walk down the path, to find a big enough tree to hide behind.

By the time I return, he's also got dressed into his black jeans, black T-shirt.

'Do you want to stay longer, and read, or draw, or whatever?' He sounds less arrogant now.

'Gabes might be awake. Let's go back.'

'As you will.' That wry, laconic smile flits over his face. He leads the way along the path. He stops near a tree, peers down into the stream. 'There's an old pike lives in here somewhere. Do you know that Ted Hughes poem?

'No.'

'I'll find it for you, when we get home.'

It's clouded over. Looks like rain again. At the stile, Theo climbs over first then holds out his hand to help me down, even though I don't need help. He keeps hold of my hand the rest of the way, as far as the house track, and I let him. There's something powerful about him: a dark kind of magic, winding me in.

Just before we arrive at the house, he lets go of my hand, and looks directly into my eyes. 'Lucky Gabes. I wish I'd found you first.' He turns away, walks down to the courtyard and into the house, before I can challenge him.

Found me? As if I'm some sort of object, lying around waiting to be discovered! But despite that, his words leave me feeling – what, exactly? Excited, I think. As if I've got some sort of power or magic of my own, now, to match his.

* * *

Maddie's cooking in the kitchen. She looks up as we come in. 'Nice swim?'

'Yes, thanks,' I say. 'Freezing cold but still delicious. How's Gabes?'

'Awake, bored. Watching some film. Go and find him. He'll be glad to see you.'

Theo doesn't speak. He goes straight out of the kitchen. I listen to his feet thumping upstairs.

Gabes looks very fed up. He flicks the remote to turn off the film.

I sit down at the end of the sofa. 'Are you feeling better?'

'You were ages,' he says.

'You were sleeping. I didn't think you'd mind.'

He flicks the film back on. I watch with him for a while. 'I need to hang out my wet things,' I say. He nods without looking at me.

I rinse out my swimsuit at the kitchen sink. 'Wring it out well, then put it to dry in the utility room,' Maddie says. She smiles. 'I'm assuming you're staying for supper, Freya? And you're welcome to stay over, tonight. Laura's room's free. Or I can take you home later, if you prefer?'

Nick comes in with the twins, one on each arm. Phoebe stretches her arms out towards me and makes little crowing sounds. She can't talk yet.

I'm absurdly pleased. 'Hey, Phoebe!' I say, taking her from Nick. Her small body is so warm and light. She hardly weighs a thing. Her head, downy soft, nestles under my chin.

'I'd love to stay,' I say to Maddie. 'Thanks. I'll call

Mum.' I pass Phoebe back to Nick, so I can use my phone. I take it into the hallway.

Mum isn't there, so I leave a message on the answer-phone. I go back into the kitchen. 'Where am I, exactly? This house, I mean? So I can tell my parents.'

Nick laughs. 'Home Farm. The village is Southfield. We're a mile from the village, though.' He opens a bottle of wine, pours a glass for himself and one for Maddie. 'Freya?'

I shake my head. 'No thanks.'

I help lay the table.

'Would you be a love and go and see if there are any courgettes in the kitchen garden?' Maddie asks me. 'And spinach. Enough for eight. Thanks, darling.'

I go back to the sitting-room door. 'Gabes? Want to come with me, to pick stuff? You can practise with your crutches!' I mean to be encouraging, but he gives me such a withering look I'm happy to leave him behind.

I'm used to pottering in Gramps' vegetable garden, helping him. This one is much more overgrown and unruly. I find a handful of courgettes under the big star-shaped leaves, and then start cutting spinach. Something makes me look up. Theo's standing in the doorway to the walled garden, lurking there in the shadow. Not exactly creepy, but a bit . . . But perhaps I'm just imagining things because he comes over and is ordinary enough.

'Spinach goes to a mush when it's cooked. So you need loads,' he says.

'I know.'

'I found that poem for you. *Pike.*'

'Thanks.'

'Are you staying?'

'Yes.'

'Good.'

I don't say anything.

He starts asking me questions. 'So, Freya. You still at school?'

'No, college. I'm doing A levels there. That's how I know Gabes.'

'Then what?'

'I don't know. I haven't decided.'

'University. Or travel. Like everyone does.'

I look at him. Why does he have to be sarcastic? 'Actually, Theo, no. I'd like to do something wild, and wonderful, and different. I want my life to mean something; to count. I don't want to waste it. Not any of it.'

I don't tell him why. I don't say, *when someone you love dies young, it makes you think about all these things, over and over*.

There's a long, awkward silence.

'And you? What do you want to do, Theo?'

'Write,' he says.

'Like your mother?'

'No, not like her. Not *like* anyone.'

'That's enough spinach,' I say.

He picks up the cut leaves from the path where I've laid them, and carries them into the house in both hands, like a dark green bouquet.

Just before supper, I go to find Gabes. I pick up one of the framed photographs on the piano, put it back, select another. 'Tell me who everyone is,' I say.

Most of the family group ones are fairly obvious. I peer at a particularly beautiful black-and-white photo of Maddie and Nick on their wedding day, looking totally in love and amazing. There's another wedding one with two bridesmaids that Gabes tells me are Beth and Laura. 'Nick was married before, to their mum, Lorna,' Gabes explains. 'Maddie isn't their real mother, though she's looked after them practically for ever.'

'And this one?' I hold up the square photo of the thin-faced little girl with short dark hair, the one picture that doesn't fit with the others.

'Bridie, when she was about six.' He starts hobbling to the door.

Nick's calling us from the kitchen: supper is ready and everyone's starving. But I linger a moment longer, staring at the girl in the photograph. *This is her. I'm face to face with Bridie* . . . I study her face; look into her dark eyes. But of course there's nothing there, nothing you can see, that is; nothing that says what will happen to her later . . .

'Freya?' Gabes calls.

'Coming.' Carefully, I put the photo back between the others and go through to the kitchen.

We take our places at the table. Everyone's there except Laura, this time. Maddie has cooked an enormous fish pie. Theo watches me across the table, but I keep my eyes on my food, and on Gabes, and let the conversations waft over my head. Someone's bought an injured fox into the surgery, Nick's saying. It will need a quieter place to recuperate: he might bring it back to the house next week, if Maddie doesn't mind . . .

Afterwards, Gabes practises going upstairs with crutches. I walk along the landing to find Beth bathing the twins. She's red-faced and shiny from the steam. She sits on the floor, keeping an eye on both babies and playing with them. She wipes her hair back from her hot face and sits back for a moment. 'Don't ever have twins!' she says, but laughing at the same time, and I know she doesn't really mean it. She loves those babies to bits.

She stands up, stretches out her back. 'Watch them for me, while I get their pyjamas?'

I take her place on the floor. Phoebe's pouring water from one plastic beaker to another, while Erin pushes a blue and yellow plastic whale to make it go under the bath water. Each time it pops back up she laughs. It's unsinkable, that little toy whale. I take a small blue boat from the basket of toys and float it. It tips sideways. Not an unsinkable boat, then. The brief, painful thought of my brother, Joe, catches me unawares.

Beth hangs the pyjamas over the warm towel rail; one pink and white pair, one blue and yellow. 'Thanks, Freya. You OK?'

I nod.

'Gabes isn't his normal self. It's his foot, it's nothing to do with you.'

'I know.'

She smiles.

* * *

I find Gabes stretched out on his bed, listening to music.

I sit next to him for a while, but he seems so remote, listening to music on headphones, making no effort to talk to me, that in the end I get up and go back downstairs. He hardly seems to notice.

Piano music is drifting from the sitting room. I follow the sound. Theo's playing something haunting and rather lovely. I read the name from the music book on the piano stand: *Trois Gnossiennes*, by Erik Satie. Nick and Kit are engrossed in a game of chess, and Maddie's sitting in the window seat, reading. Family life, I think. This is what it's supposed to be like.

I pick up a book from the pile on the side table, and start to read the beginning. It's called *The Behaviour of Moths*, but it's a novel, about two crazy sisters. Every so often I look up at Theo, and one time, he's looking straight back at me, and that feeling comes again, something running between us, a little bit dark, and edgy, and exciting.

Maddie turns on more lamps as it gets dark outside. She goes over to the bookshelves and pulls out a big hardback art book for me to look at. 'You might like this, Freya. Do you know her work? I think she's a wonderful painter. Very underrated. You know St Ives, I expect, in Cornwall. She lived there for a while.'

Winifred Nicholson. I leaf through the pages. I've seen some of the paintings before: *Gate to the Isles* is pretty famous, but there are others I haven't seen, and yes, Maddie's right, I do love them. The colours, and the emotion that they evoke. How, exactly? I'm not sure. I stare for ages at one called *Dawn Chorus*.

Theo stops playing, and stretches out on the rug, reading too. It's quiet except for the sound of wooden chess pieces on the board, and heavy sighs from Kit as Nick steadily and inexorably defeats him. The almost-silence of people in a room, all happily absorbed in something: I love it.

At last, Maddie looks up from her book. 'Time for bed, for me. Shall I show you Laura's room, Freya?'

I nod. I take the art book with me upstairs, and pad behind Maddie, past the rows of doors, where Beth and the twins are already sleeping. We go past Gabes' room, and Maddie pauses there, listens, opens the door and closes it again very quietly.

'Fast asleep. Good. That's when the healing happens: while you're sleeping. Like *growing* does, when you're a child.'

We take another step down, turn a corner. I've not been this far before, or seen the narrow wooden steps leading up to an attic bedroom.

'There you go. I put a towel on the bed. Help yourself to anything you need.' She hugs me briefly, as if she were my own mother. 'Sleep well, Freya.'

I step carefully up to the attic, with its sloping walls and narrow single bed, cream covers, cream rug, a single wooden chair. A green-covered book is lying on the pillow: Ted Hughes, *Selected Poems*, and a thin slip of paper marks page 59. A shiver runs down my spine; I don't know why. I pick up the towel and go back down to the bathroom for a shower.

I make myself wait till I'm actually in bed, under the white duvet, before I open the book. I read the poem about the pike, first, then one about an otter, and a fox. The poems are full of darkness, and sounds, and something disturbing that I can't quite fathom.

I find a message from Mum on my phone. She's got mine, she hopes I'm having a good time, she'll see me tomorrow. And there's one from Miranda: **How's it going???? Tell all!!**

I text her back: **We had a bike accident! Gabes broke his foot. I'm staying over, in his sister's room,** and then I turn off my phone because I don't want to speak to anyone right now. Even the tiny clicking sounds of texting sound loud in the deep silence of this ancient, solid house.

I dream of St Ailla. The colours are as bright as a Pre-Raphaelite painting. In the dream, I'm walking across the sandbar at high tide: it's a neap tide so there's a strip of sand a metre or so wide at the top of the bar. If it were a spring tide, the sea would cover it completely, and the water would be rushing and swirling and eddying in dangerous currents. But no: I can walk right the way across to the next island without getting wet feet. At the far end of the bar I scramble over big stones and stinky seaweed, on to the short turf path that runs between tall bracken, up to the top of Gara. The island is uninhabited except by birds: black-backed gulls wheel over it, calling incessantly, and dive-bombing you if you come too close to their nesting places on the rocks. I cross to the other side, in the lee of the wind, and sit for a while against the huge lichen-covered boulders at the edge of the cliff. Oystercatchers with their bright orange legs and black-and-white plumage make their piping song and fly off as I walk down to their beach. The sun's prickly hot on my skin. I strip off, walk out into the water and begin to swim. Ahead, there's nothing but blue sea, on and on to the line of the horizon where the dark blue meets the paler blue of sky. I am utterly at peace, swimming into the wild blue.

I wake up, the dream vivid in my head, full of that sense of peace, and purposefulness. In the dream there was no uncertainty, no muddled feelings. I lie in the darkness for ages, and then I switch on the bedside light, get out of bed to find my notebook and a pen, and begin to draw. I'm drawing from the dream, and from the memory of the real place, vividly alive for me. But I'm drawing as if I am an observer, watching myself in the scene: a series of sketches like a storyboard, or a cartoon strip. I draw fast, instinctively, without stopping to think. The drawings retrace my journey across the island, but at the top of the cliff I stop and there's something else there, something I didn't see the first time: a dead bird, a patch of soft feathers around the torn corpse of a brown speckled hawk, its ribcage stripped open to reveal the red raw inside. The girl changes, too. She isn't me, I realise after a while. She has short dark hair, and she looks the way I imagine little Bridie from the photograph might have looked when she was older: about eighteen or nineteen.

I check the time. It's three o'clock, the dead time of the night, the time when people who are dying actually die, when the life force is at its lowest ebb. I switch off the light, and I drift in the darkness, back towards sleep, until it's properly morning and the house begins to wake.

Ten

Beth offers to give me a lift home. Neither Gabes nor Theo are up, but I've had breakfast and helped Maddie let the hens out, and played with the babies all before ten o'clock, and I'm ready to go.

She drives slowly and carefully along the lanes. She looks different this morning, I think: lighter and happier. Or perhaps it's just that she's driving, and not with the children: we've got the windows open and a CD playing in the car. She turns up the volume. 'Listen to this one,' she says. 'My favourite.'

It's a song about being free, and close to the one you love. '*Closer to heaven, and closer to you*,' Beth sings along. The lyrics will stay in my head all day.

'Life is so much easier when I stay at Home Farm,' Beth says. 'You can't imagine how difficult it is, sometimes, on my own with the children all day. It's turning me into some kind of monster. No wonder Will doesn't want to come home to us at the end of the day.'

I'm embarrassed. I don't really want to hear all the

details of Beth's marriage problems. I don't know what to say.

'So, did you have a nice time? In spite of grumpy Gabes?'

'Yes. I love being there, too,' I say. 'My own home's a bit . . . quiet, I suppose. A bit empty.'

'*Quiet* sounds heavenly, to me!'

'It's the wrong sort of quiet,' I say.

Beth glances at me. 'I'm sorry. Tactless of me. I've just remembered what Gabes told us. About your brother.'

I don't say anything. I'm wondering what Gabes has said, and to whom. I don't like people feeling sorry for me.

'You'll have to tell me where to go, in a minute,' Beth says, as we turn on to the ring road. 'I know the general area, but not exactly where your street is.'

I give directions and she stops at the top of the hill for me to get out.

'Thanks so much, Beth. It's really kind of you.'

'My pleasure. Any time, really. Thanks for helping me with the babes, too.' She scrabbles about in her handbag and finds a pen and scrap of paper. 'My mobile,' she says. 'In case you need a lift or anything, while Gabes is in plaster and can't drive the bike.'

'Thanks, Beth!' I watch her turn the car and drive off, before I walk down the hill to my house. I really like her. I wish I'd had an older sister, like her.

Dad's car is outside. He's back from his conference.

The back door's wide open; the kitchen smells of coffee and toast. Through the window I see them – my parents – at the table, talking together. Mum's laughing. I don't disturb them. It's rare to see Mum laugh like that, or looking as if she's feeling close to Dad, happy even. At one point two summers ago I thought they might be about to separate, but they didn't, and I am so glad about it I find myself wanting to do everything I can to keep them close. Sometimes I worry that being with me reminds them too much about the child who is missing. That having no children around might be easier than just one.

I go upstairs instead and lie on my bed. I'm tired, from being awake so much of the night. Later, I'll do my work for college, and phone Miranda. Later.

Monday morning. Art. Our lecturer, Jeanette, is going round looking at everyone's preliminary studies. I spread my notebooks out on the table ready, plus a stack of paintings I've been working on: small watercolours, mostly, apart from the one I did yesterday, which I put at the bottom because I think it is the best one, and I want her to see it last. All yesterday afternoon I worked fast, intuitively, painting the scene in the dream: the girl swimming into the blue, viewed from a high vantage point on the lichen-covered rock, with the space of air and light between.

Jeanette's face doesn't give anything away. She picks up the notebooks first, flicks through the pages, turns them the right way round where I've worked over two pages, sideways on. She leafs through the paintings, until she reaches the sea one. She spends a long time studying it. She looks at me. 'This one, this is very interesting. The viewpoint, and your use of colour, and the sense of flow. As if you were painting at the scene, very fast.'

I breathe out, relieved.

'But it seems to be more about harmony than discord. Of itself, it's very good, Freya. The quality of light and air is beautiful. Keep working like this. Do some more paintings. Start to think about how you might interpret the theme more explicitly.' She flips back through some of the drawings, stops when she gets to the one with the dead bird. 'This, for example. Could the hawk be part of the painting? The element of discord in the scene? Or is that too obvious? Perhaps it could be connected in some way to the figure of the girl?'

'I'll think some more,' I say.

Gabes isn't in college, and although I'm not surprised, I miss him at the breaks. I text him, to see how he is, and he texts back, briefly. He's bored, he says. When Miranda and I catch up at lunchtime and I describe my weekend I don't mention Theo, because that makes everything too complicated, somehow, which means I leave out quite a lot of the detail. I wonder at myself, later: since when have I become so secretive?

Gabes is away from college all week. He texts me back when I send him texts, but he never phones or anything. So I'm not sure what to think.

Now it's Friday, after school, and I've brought a mug of tea and my art notebooks outside to the garden table, partly because I want to make the most of this last bit of sunshine, and partly because the house seemed so empty and lonely when I got home. Neither Mum nor Dad is back from work, even though it's after six.

All this week, I've thought about Gabes, but I've also been thinking about Theo. I know I shouldn't: he'll be going back to Oxford for the new term any day now, and it's disloyal to Gabes, even if nothing has really happened between Gabes and me, yet. Perhaps that's the trouble: we're friends, but not really anything more than that, even though he doesn't have a girlfriend, and we've been spending lots of time together, and I've been to his house twice . . . and Miranda says it's blindingly obvious that he likes me. I think of us lying side by side on his bed, last Saturday evening. It was me who got up and left, wasn't it? But he didn't seem bothered. He went on listening to his music, as if he didn't mind either way. And he still hasn't phoned. He's never the one to send a message first: he just replies to mine. But then, maybe he's just in pain, and a bit out of it . . .

When I think of Theo, it's different: exciting, and a bit *wrong*, as if instinctively I know it won't be good for me, being with him.

'You need to make the first move, if Gabes isn't going to,' Miranda said, when we were having lunch together at the Boston café. 'Why should it always be the bloke who has to do that? Perhaps he's shy, or he's not sure how you will react. You need to make it more obvious that you want him to. So he's absolutely clear it's what you want.'

But is it? That's the real problem, I slowly realise. I'm not clear, even with myself. I keep telling myself it doesn't matter, that none of this is that important, anyway, in the grand scheme of things. Why shouldn't I be friends with both of them? They are brothers, after all.

Friendship. Is that what I'm wanting, really, with both? Is that all? Is it enough? Or is it the family, all of them, that I want to be a part of? My need to belong somewhere? Because my family is just too . . . small? It doesn't feel like a family at all, any more.

Too much thinking does my head in. I open my box of pastels and start to draw. I do what Jeanette says: pay attention to the object, look properly, as if you have never seen it before. Draw what is actually there, not what you think is there, and keep the connection: the eye, and the hand, moving across the page. An edge of table, and the back of a chair, and a plant in a pot: a geranium with leaves that smell of lemon, and tiny white flowers. The smell is part of it, but how can you show that, in a painting? Through colour? Association? The drawing lacks depth, somehow. I push the page away from me.

Mum phones: she's got a meeting after work so she's going to be late, and Dad won't be home till nine. 'Make yourself something proper for supper,' she says. 'Have some fruit and vegetables.'

'I'm sixteen, Mum. You don't need to tell me.'

The house seems even emptier now. On impulse, I phone Gabes.

My heart does a little flutter as he answers.

'Thought I'd actually speak to you,' I say. 'Instead of texting. Is your foot any better? What have you been doing today?'

'Lying around, watching crap telly, mostly,' Gabes says. 'And being bored.' There's a slight pause, before he says, 'Do you want to come over, this evening?'

'Well, yes, that would be great. But I'm not sure how I can get there . . . my parents aren't around. There's no one to give me a lift . . .'

'Hang on a minute.'

I hear him calling out to someone, and voices in the background, and then he speaks into the phone again. 'Beth can come and get you. She said she'd like to.'

'Really?'

'She wouldn't offer otherwise. You can help her out, sometime, if you want to pay her back.' I hear voices again, in the background. Gabes laughs. 'Now she's cross with me for saying that. You don't have to do anything, she says. What's your address, again? She thinks it'll take her about half an hour.'

So suddenly I'm happy, and rushing around, changing into clean jeans and top and getting my things together. Money, phone, notebook and pastels, which I then take out of the bag again, swimming things, just in case I get to stay over and it's warm enough to swim tomorrow; toothbrush, a change of top and underwear . . .

Beth texts me, to say she's at the top of the road. By the time I get there, she's turning the car round, ready. She leans across to open the door for me. 'Sling your bag on the back seat, if you can find a space!'

I push it between the twins' car seats.

'Thanks so much, Beth!' I say as I fasten the seat belt, and she drives off. I look at her, remembering what she told me last time. 'So, how's your week in Oxford been?'

'Awful,' she says. 'Don't ask. That's why I've come home again for the weekend. Will's staying in London.'

Home. Such a tiny word, and so telling. You'd expect her house in Oxford with her husband Will to be her home, but instead she uses the word for the house she grew up in, with her parents. Or rather, her dad. Maddie, I remember now, isn't her real mother, even if she's been like a mother most of her life.

Beth smiles at me. 'But I'm fine now. Just having other people around, the twins seem so much easier to look after, and happier. Gabes has been great with them this afternoon. Playing endless games of bricks and reading stories. They love him.'

She concentrates on driving for a bit, negotiating traffic on to the London Road and then over the bridge to the ring road. It's busy at this time on a Friday.

I clear my throat. 'And Theo? Is he at home this weekend?'

'Yes. His last one before uni starts up again.' She glances at me, curiously, and I wish I hadn't asked.

She turns off the lane down to the farmhouse. The green driveway isn't green any longer: the leaves on the overhanging trees have turned brown and gold. My spirits lift again. I love the first glimpse of the cobbled yard, the whitewashed walls and dipping roof, and that big wooden door into the kitchen.

Gabes must have heard the car. He comes out to meet us. 'Hey! Freya!' He hugs me, and I'm so relieved and happy I forget about the awkward moment in the car with Beth. Everyone seems pleased to see me: his mum, the twins and even Kit, on his way out somewhere. There's no sign of Theo.

'You'll be amazed how quick I am on these now!' Gabes waves one of the crutches. 'Even outside, and up and down stairs.'

I laugh. 'That's good.'

'Come and see the latest addition to the family.'

'Who's that, then?'

'The fox. Remember Dad talking about it?'

I do, vaguely. 'Where is it?'

I follow him out of the house again and across the courtyard, round the side of the house. Against the wall someone's made a small pen out of wood and wire mesh. The young fox is crouched at the back. It cowers further into the shadows, and bares its teeth in a snarl. I can just make out the bandaged leg.

'She's terrified, obviously. But we can't let her go till her leg's mended. And that'll be weeks. But we mustn't make her too tame, either, otherwise she won't readjust to being wild.'

'It seems a lot of effort,' I say, 'just for one fox.'

I'm thinking of all the dead ones you see at the side of the road, along with the squashed badgers and pheasants.

Gabes looks indignant. 'You'll be saying you believe in fox hunting, next,' he says.

'No, no, I don't! I think it's horribly cruel,' I say. 'I'm

just surprised, I suppose, about your dad going to such a lot of work for a fox. But perhaps if someone brings a creature to the vet's, they have to save it. A bit like doctors, signing that oath.'

'The Hippocratic oath.'

'Yes. About the sanctity of life. Not killing.'

'But vets have to put animals to sleep all the time. That's killing. Dad hates doing it, actually. Mum's always had a thing about taking in waifs and strays. Injured birds, that sort of thing. She does it with people too.'

'What do you mean?'

'People who need looking after a bit. You know. Like, if we had friends when we were little, and she thought they were a bit . . . neglected, or not eating enough or unhappy or whatever, she'd invite them back with us. That's what happened with Bridie.'

'What did happen, exactly?'

In all the warmth and happiness at Home Farm, it's never seemed quite right to ask more about Bridie. I've been a bit scared about it: as if her sad story might spill over and spoil everything. But I really want to know, now.

'She came to stay with us when she was about five . . .' Gabes' voice drifts, goes vague. 'Bridie's mum couldn't cope . . . Mum helped out for a while, but it was a bit of a mistake. It didn't work out so well.'

He takes a step nearer the fox.

She cringes back, but her ears are pricked up, alert, and her nose sniffing the air. And next, surprisingly, she yawns.

Gabes laughs. 'She reminds me a bit of Bridie,' he says. 'Bridie when she was older, though, a teenager. Angry, and very bored, and underneath it all, scared stiff.'

I want to ask *why*. Why was she frightened? But Gabes is hopping back the way we came. I creep forward, and crouch down so I'm at nearly the same level as the fox. Her eyes shine in the dark at the back of the cage. Her tail is curled round neatly over her toes. 'Bridie,' I whisper to her, and her ears go back and then forward again, as if she is tuning in, listening to me.

Beth's making a meal for the twins, so she can get them to bed before we all eat a proper grown-up dinner: roast chicken, potatoes roasted with garlic and rosemary, green beans, gravy, followed by home-made apple pie and cream. I'm already starving, just thinking about it.

'Want to help Phoebe?' Beth asks me.

'Of course!' I settle down at the table, next to the high chair, and try to spoon baby dinner into Phoebe's mouth before she turns her head or grabs the spoon. She wants to feed herself, really, and Beth wants to encourage that so it's all a bit of a messy slow business. In the end we play the animal noises game: *one spoonful for the tiger, mmm, yum yum. Roar like a tiger. One mouthful for the dog . . .*

Maddie comes in and out of the kitchen, checking on the roast, washing things up, making encouraging remarks to the babies about how well they're doing and how gorgeous they are. It makes me feel as if I'm doing a good job too. I wonder if that's why she does it, partly: to make Beth feel nice. Like, to show her she *is* a good mother.

Nick arrives home from his surgery. He washes his hands at the sink. 'Hello, Freya! Seen our fox?'

'Yes. Gabes showed me.'

'She's doing well,' Nick says. 'As she starts getting better, we'll have to make sure she can't get out and have a go at the hens.'

'She looked too scared for that,' I say.

'Appearances are deceptive,' Nick says. 'Especially with foxes! They are just as clever and cunning in real life as they are in stories. They can wreak havoc.'

'Dinner in about thirty minutes,' Maddie says.

We untie the babies' bibs and lift them out of the high chairs. Maddie starts clearing up the mess.

'Can I help with bath and bedtime?' I ask Beth.

Gabes gives me a quick look I can't quite interpret. Possibly, *why?* I'm not sure why myself, even . . .

I go ahead anyway.

'Come on then,' I say to Phoebe. 'Up we go!'

Once we've finally got them settled in Beth's room, I tiptoe out and close the door behind me. The delicious smell of roast meat is drifting up from the kitchen. I can hear music playing from one of the bedrooms. A ballad: something sad and mournful.

On the landing, I hesitate for a moment. The music's coming from the room next to Gabes'. Theo's?

By the time I get down to the kitchen the table is

laid ready and Maddie's serving the meal. She looks up. 'Good. Is Beth nearly ready?'

'Yes,' I say. 'I think so.'

'Where's Theo?' she asks. 'Anyone seen him? Someone go and see if he's in his room, But go quietly, in case the twins are just dropping off. Don't just yell up the stairs!'

Gabes starts gathering up his crutches. 'Not you!' Maddie says. 'You can't do anything quietly on those!'

I look towards Nick: he's busy reading a letter or something at the dresser.

'I'll go,' I say.

I tap on his door, too quietly at first, what with the music, and then say his name.

The music goes quiet; he opens the door. 'Freya!'

'Supper's ready,' I tell him. I stand there, waiting.

'Aren't you coming in?'

I shake my head. 'Maddie says come now, to eat. It's all served up ready.'

'What are you frightened of, Freya?' Theo half smiles, mocking me.

'Nothing,' I say quickly. I turn away, and at that moment he reaches out and pulls me towards him, and he kisses me, before I know what's happening or can stop him. And at that precise second, Beth comes out of her room, and sees us. She turns away, goes on down the landing to the stairs.

I'm furious with Theo. I pull away, my heart thumping, but I'm too shocked and embarrassed to make a fuss or say anything. Instead I just stupidly follow

Beth down to the kitchen. *It's not what you think! It wasn't my fault*, I want to explain, but there's no time, she's already joining the rest of the family in the bright, steamy kitchen, and in any case, even I can see that anything I say would sound ridiculous. But I still feel awful, even though it wasn't my fault.

What was he *thinking*?

Theo comes downstairs eventually, after we've all started eating, looking strange: dark-eyed, talking too fast, showing off. I try not to look at him.

Gabes sighs. His earlier good mood begins to evaporate.

Beth is watching all three of us, especially me.

'You don't have much of an appetite,' Maddie says, eyeing me over her glasses.

'That explains how she stays so slim and lovely!' Nick says cheerfully. 'Unlike me.' He pats his round belly.

'Stop talking about Freya like that. You are both so embarrassing.' Gabes sounds defensive. 'Take no notice, Freya.'

Beth clears the plates and brings the apple pie to the table. 'What's everyone doing tomorrow?' she says. 'Theo's packing, presumably?' She looks over and glares at him.

'I might have a last swim,' he says, nonchalantly. 'I've got all Sunday for packing.'

'Don't leave it till the last minute,' Beth says. 'If I'm taking you, you'll need to be ready by three at the latest. I mean it.'

'Stop stressing,' Theo says. 'What's the matter with you?'

Beth bites her lip.

Maddie intervenes, skilfully. 'I shall be cleaning out the hens first thing, so any help gratefully received, and then doing a bit of tidying up in the garden. I need to do a big shop, too; we've got people coming for the evening.'

'Who?' Gabes asks.

'Kate and Tim.'

'Dad's sister and her partner,' Gabes explains to me. 'Sorry, yet more family.'

'Extended family,' Beth says. 'Dad's family, mainly. He's the *prolific* one.'

After supper, we all help clear the dishes, and then Gabes and I take some leftover chicken out to the fox.

As soon as I open the makeshift door she comes rushing and snapping at my hand. I drop the meat and shut the door again quickly and fasten the catch. 'She's starving!' I say. 'Or desperate to get out, perhaps.'

Gabes doesn't hear me. He's gone back into the courtyard and is staring up at the sky. 'There are loads of stars, tonight,' he says. 'Look, Freya!'

They are nothing compared to the stars you see at St Ailla, where there are no street lights, no roads or cars, hardly any houses, even, but I don't say that to Gabes. Instead, I point out the constellations I know, and he shows me which planets are extra bright this time of year. He stands close behind me, and I lean back ever so slightly, against him, but nothing else happens. He doesn't put his arms round me, or kiss me, or anything . . . and then Maddie yells at us to close the back door and we go back inside.

Gabes and I go upstairs to his room. We walk past Theo's shut door. We sit on the bed together because there isn't anywhere else, really, and in any case he needs to rest up his leg. He asks me about college, and I talk a bit about my sea painting.

'Tell me some more about Bridie,' I ask him.

'Why are you so interested in her?' Gabes says.

'I don't know . . . I suppose because of being on the train, and then the connection with your family . . . and because . . . I want to understand how such a thing could happen.'

He doesn't speak for a while.

'Do you mind?' I ask.

'No. I don't know what to tell you, though. What do you want to know, exactly?'

'Her story, I suppose. What happened to her.'

'OK. Well, I'll tell you my version. Theo would have a different take on it.'

Eleven

'The first time Bridie came to stay she must have been five or six; I don't really remember: I was only about three. I think it was because her mother needed a break – she was a friend of Beth and Laura's mum, Lorna. Bridie's mother had lots of problems with alcohol, drugs and that; she wasn't coping. Lorna helped out when she could, and somehow Mum got roped in too – Dad was still friends with Lorna in those days; he had to be, for Beth and Laura's sake, so Mum knew Lorna too. Bridie was the same age as Theo. Mum thought they could play together. Which they did. They were quite close.

'After that, she'd come from time to time – the holidays, mostly, and some weekends. She was already struggling at school. I can vaguely remember Mum trying to help her learn to read: sitting with Bridie at the table, helping her sound out words, or getting her to talk about the pictures. I remember that because I was already beginning to read, even though I was two years younger, and Theo was streets ahead – reading proper chapter books by himself. Mum thought Bridie might be dyslexic, though the school didn't agree: they thought it was emotional, or something.'

Gabes looks at me. 'Are you sure you want to hear all this?'

'Yes. I'm interested. Really.'

'OK. Well, Bridie started being more troublesome. Naughty. She started nicking stuff: small things, our toys, bits of Lego and stuff from Beth's and Laura's rooms: doll's house furniture, or hair beads, or rubbers – silly little things, really. And Mum would find them in her pockets, when she washed her clothes, but Bridie would always lie, deny taking them. Mum said it was a sign of Bridie's unhappiness, and needing love and other things that were missing in her life, so she tried to be understanding and loving, not cross. But that made us cross instead – like there was one set of rules for Bridie, and another for the rest of us children. Plus, it was our stuff getting stolen! And Mum explaining to us *why* didn't make much difference. As far as we were concerned it wasn't fair.

'Mum said if we were loving and patient, little by little we'd win her round: Bridie would begin to trust, and feel secure, and then she'd stop stealing our things. But we didn't feel like being loving. Bridie was mean, and spiteful. She'd pinch you, or pull your hair, or say horrible things. One time, Mum caught her just about to push Kit out of an open upstairs window. It really scared Mum. So, after that it took up more and more of Mum's time, watching out in case something else happened. And Mum had underestimated

Bridie – the extent to which she'd been *damaged.* Mum was – is – too optimistic. She always thinks that if you are loving and kind, that's enough.'

'Isn't it?'

'No. I don't think so, now. It didn't work with Bridie. Or maybe we didn't try hard enough.' Gabes shrugs.

I'm thinking about what he's said. Putting a hurt child into the middle of this big, close, loving family: wouldn't that make a difference? Surely it would.

'Mum wouldn't give up on Bridie. She went on inviting her for holidays and weekends, right up till Bridie was a teenager, and really going off the rails. She stopped going to school at all; she got done for shoplifting, she went round with all the wrong sort of people – mostly older than her, and into smoking cannabis and worse things, living in squats. And she stopped coming here altogether.

'Bridie got even thinner, and more sick-looking. Sometimes Mum would meet her in Bristol for a coffee or buy her lunch and I think she probably gave her money. Sometimes Theo went with Mum, to meet Bridie. I'm not really sure why. He was kind of fascinated by her, and the life she led, or what she represented, perhaps. The other side of life. The *shadow* side. And when Theo started to meet up with Bridie by himself, after she moved again, to Devon, that's when Mum got really worried.'

The cat scratches at the bedroom door: Gabes stops talking while he lets her in. She jumps on to the bed and starts kneading the covers with her paws, turning round and round to make a sort of nest to curl into.

The phone rings downstairs. We hear footsteps padding upstairs and along the landing.

It's Maddie. 'Freya?' she calls out. 'I'm driving into town shortly to collect Kit. Do you want a lift home?'

I hesitate, hoping Gabes is going to invite me to stay over. But he just sits there. He doesn't say anything, and I can't really ask, can I?

So I call back to Maddie. 'Yes, please.'

'Five minutes, then.'

I glance at the time. It's ten twenty-five. I'm desperate for Gabes to get to the end of Bridie's story before I have to go. 'Why was your mum worried?' I ask. 'About Theo?'

'Theo was having a hard time. Mum was worried he'd get sucked into Bridie's world. *Underworld*, rather.' Gabes stretches, and the cat looks up and yawns at us both, before turning over to let Gabes stroke the silky white fur under her chin. 'She's definitely pregnant.'

For a second I think he means Bridie, before I realise he's talking about the cat.

There's obviously more to say about Theo and Bridie, but Gabes has had enough, or is fed up with me asking, or something. In any case, my five minutes are up.

I sigh. 'I better go downstairs. Maddie will be waiting. Thanks for inviting me over. Sorry if I made you talk too much.'

Gabes shrugs. 'I'll be back at college on Monday,' he says. 'Dad's going to take me in. So I'll see you then. We can have lunch together, or coffee, whatever.'

I swing my legs back off the bed, lean over and kiss his cheek. 'Yes. Bye, Gabes.'

I walk slowly down our road, thinking about what Gabes has just told me about Bridie. What could have happened to make her like that in the first place? I think about Gabes, too. I'm even more confused about him now. I guess he just want us to be friends, after all. Nothing more than that.

Instead of an amazing weekend at Home Farm, I've now got two days on my own with nothing planned. Plus, I feel really stupid, taking my overnight things like that. I'd die if anyone knew. And it's Theo's last weekend. I won't see him again.

The lights are on, and I hear music as soon as I open the front door. Mum's got the sewing machine out on the big kitchen table. I can't remember the last time she did any sewing.

'What are you making?' I kiss the top of her head and she puts one arm round my waist.

'Curtains.' She holds out the thick blue cotton. 'Like the colour?'

'Yes. Gorgeous. Sea colour.'

'For the spare room. I'm going to turn it into a study, for me.'

I look at her, surprised. 'Studying what?'

'Garden design. Landscape gardening. So I can move out of boring office work altogether, eventually. What do you reckon?'

'It's a brilliant idea, Mum. What does Dad say?'

'He's thrilled. He might even be able to put work in

my direction, when I've qualified. People with new houses might want a newly designed garden, too.'

I fill the kettle. 'Tea, Mum?'

'Not for me. Just had one. So, how was your evening? Where've you been, exactly?'

'Gabes' house.'

Mum grins. 'You've been seeing him a lot, recently. Am I going to be allowed to meet him?'

I sigh. 'Yes. I guess. There's no big deal. He's just a friend at college. I like his family. It's nice, being there with lots of people. And they cook these big family dinners . . . it's all very homey and nice.'

Mum winces.

I realise immediately I've hurt her. It's not her fault our home is so empty and quiet. That so many of her and Dad's friends just seemed to vanish away, after Joe died, as if grief was contagious. Or simply too hard to witness, perhaps.

Mum starts packing the sewing things away for the night. 'Your friend Danny phoned again, but he didn't leave a message. I said I'd tell you. And Evie sends her love. We had a lovely long conversation. She's missing you. She was wondering whether we might all go over at half-term, or Christmas.'

'How's Gramps?'

'Much the same. A little more muddled. But happy enough, Evie says.'

I take my tea upstairs to my room. I can hear Dad sloshing around in the bath as I go past. He's listening to the radio, which means he'll be there for ages.

I stand in the doorway of the spare room. This

would be Joe's room, if Joe were still alive. Except not really: we wouldn't have left the old house, with the garden leading down to the canal, if Joe hadn't had his accident. We'd be living there still. *What might have been . . .* But I have to stop thinking like that. We all do.

That night, I have the weirdest dream. I'm in a sort of open-sided car, no seat belt, being driven by Theo over a steep green hill, at a precarious angle, much too fast. To my left, the hill drops away to a cliff, and beyond that is the bluest sea. I try and persuade him to slow down but he won't take any notice of me. I wake up too hot, my heart beating too fast. It's still dark, no sound from the street yet, so I guess it's three or four o'clock. I make myself breathe deeply, counting, in, out, slowly, to calm myself down.

Theo.

Bridie.

Me.

That pull towards darkness, danger, death that I have . . . my fascination with it . . . what is that all about, really?

Bridie's story is just sad. What's even sadder is that there are so many stories like hers. You only have to watch telly for a week, or listen to the news, to see how much sadness there is in the world. Dad and I watched a programme the other evening about some children taken hostage at a school in Beslan, Russia, back in 2004. Hundreds of people died. The cemetery was full of children's graves, headstones with photographs: children frozen in time, forever five, or eight, or eleven years old. The boys who survived thought all the time about violence and revenge. The girls were different. Quietly, deeply depressed.

Something else struck me. All the children said that they must have survived for a reason. They would do something special and amazing with their life. They would make sure that they would be *extraordinary* adults.

I saw in them something which I recognise in myself: that feeling about how precious life is. About how not to take it for granted, ever.

Which is exactly what Bridie didn't have, did she? Bridie gave up. She lost hope. And why was that? That's the mystery, for me. The thing I need to understand.

Twelve

It's properly autumn now. Our sunny, golden September is just a memory. There have been huge storms: Evie sent me a letter describing the October gales which cut off the island for a week, and washed up the carcass of a rare Sowerby's beaked whale on Periglis beach. She enclosed a photo, taken on Gramps' old Leica camera. Twelve feet long, female. They are normally a deepwater species: it's very unusual to see them.

I wish I could be there. But it's not practical, not even for half-term; it's too expensive, and too likely that bad weather will mean I can't get back on time for college, and Dad won't hear of that.

A postcard arrives, from Oxford. Theo's message, written in fine italic handwriting in black ink, is a puzzle.

Cycled to Binsey.

Wildness and wet.

Visit?

He's written his address in tiny writing along the top of the card, and a mobile number.

It doesn't take me long on the computer to track down Binsey, a place near Oxford, and another link takes me to a poem by Gerard Manley Hopkins, called 'Binsey Poplars', and then, another hop, to 'Inversnaid' and the line about *wildness and wet*. But I still don't know what he's going on about.

And *visit?*

Me, does he mean?

I prop the postcard on my bookshelf, next to Evie's whale. The picture is of something called the Radcliffe Camera, which is nothing to do with cameras actually, but a circular building made of stone, with a famous library inside. Theo's drawn a stick man in one of the little windows, and an arrow pointing to it. *T.F., reading.*

Miranda comes round after college, Friday afternoon, so we can plan the weekend. Our college tutor says we've all got to start thinking about whether we are going to apply for university next year, and Miranda's wondering about visiting Edinburgh, for one of those Open Days that universities put on.

'And then it would be fine to email Jamie, wouldn't it? Without coming over too keen? Just friendly, seeing as I was going to be in Edinburgh anyway.'

It takes me a minute to catch up. 'Jamie?'

'The guy I met on holiday. Who's a student in Edinburgh? Remember? Freya! Concentrate!'

'Sorry, Yes, Only, I thought you'd moved on, you know, to Charlie.'

Miranda gives a hollow laugh. 'Well, that's dead

and buried. He's made that perfectly clear. He's married to his music.'

I laugh. 'He doesn't deserve you, anyway. He only wants an admiring audience. You don't want to be yet another groupie.'

'You've never said that before!'

'I know, well, you wouldn't have listened before.'

'So? What do you reckon?' She gets up off my bed and turns on my computer on the desk in front of the window. She goes on her Facebook, to show me her holiday photos again.

Jamie looks nice enough. 'What's he doing at uni?'

'Physics.'

'Hmmm. Well, why not? You can but try. But don't actually stay at his place; get a room in the youth hostel. Just arrange to have coffee or something.'

'How sensible you are, Freya.'

'Only cos I care about you!'

'What about you? You going to visit some art colleges?'

'No, I don't think so.' And then I see Theo's card on my table and the words just come out of my mouth. 'I might go to Oxford for a look around.'

'Dead posh! You could check out Cambridge, too.'

'I don't know; maybe it's a stupid idea. Way out of my league. I'd have to get three As!'

'Which you will.'

'It's probably not my kind of place, anyway. I don't even know if you can do Art there.'

'Which is why you have to go and see! Sorted. Now: tonight. Film first, then round to Tabby's place?'

We look at what's on at the multiplex. Miranda starts phoning round, to get everyone to come with us. I go downstairs to make us something to eat.

It wasn't really a serious idea, when I first said it. But over the next days it begins to seem quite a sensible thing; something I might actually do. I look up the colleges and the trains to get there. I tell Dad and he starts waxing lyrical about Oxford – medieval buildings, all that history. So I write a postcard to Theo – I spend ages choosing which – I decide on a painting by Edward Hopper, called *Nighthawks:* gloomy and atmospheric, a single man at a bar at night.

Dear Theo, I'm coming to Oxford second weekend in November for Open Day visits at Oxford Brookes and Ruskin. Suggest a café if you want to meet me on the Saturday some time. Freya.

I hesitate. Do I put a kiss? I decide not. Just my mobile number.

There's nothing witty or clever about my message. I stick on a stamp, and post it on my way to college before I change my mind.

Thirteen

I've been working on my sea paintings. It would be so much easier if I were actually there, on the island. I've got my sketchbooks, and my memories of it all, from so many summer visits, but it's still not the same. I have a habit of seeing what I want to see, what I want to remember: an idealised landscape. I blot out the rest. And that's not going to work for this project.

My eye catches the whale photo, dusty and fading in the sunlight. On impulse, I phone Evie.

It's funny, listening to the telephone ring and being able to see exactly where everything is in that house, imagining Evie in the sitting room reading, and Gramps pottering in the greenhouse, or bringing in the crab pots; knowing the particular way the house smells – the faint salty fishy tang from cooked crab – hearing that background sound of the sea pounding the rocky shore.

'Hello?' Evie's voice comes, bright and full of energy, like she always is.

'It's me,' I say.

'Freya! How lovely! How are you? We've missed you

so much this time. Did you get the photo? It's been very exciting here, what with the whale and all the fuss it brought.'

'The photo is why I phoned. I mean, to talk to you and everything, but I wondered if you had more photos like that?'

I explain about my art project, and Evie makes encouraging noises, and she says she'll send all the photos she took, all thirty-six on the film.

'Can you send copies?' I say. 'So I can keep them and don't have to worry about them getting spoiled. I'd like to be able to do things with them, like stick them in my notebooks or cut out bits.'

'Of course,' Evie says. 'It'll take a few days, mind you. I'll go over to Main Island tomorrow on the early boat, if the wind isn't too strong. We've had the most magnificent storms!'

'I wish I'd been there for them,' I say.

'The storms brought lots of unusual birds, too,' Evie says, 'as well as the whale. Rare species, blown off course on their migrations. We've had a lovely time with the field glasses. Now, Gramps would love a word. Have you got time?'

I hear their voices, and Gramps fumbles over the receiver as he takes it from Evie. 'Sweetheart,' he says. 'How's tricks?'

'I'm fine,' I tell him. 'The weather's changed. No more river swimming. How are you, Gramps?'

'Fair to middling. Are you studying hard, Freya? You want to make the most of it.' I can hear the smile in his voice. 'What are you reading just now?'

I tell him about *The Mill on the Floss*, and then I remember the Ted Hughes poems, so I mention those, too. Gramps loves poetry.

'Not my cup of tea, Hughes. That funny business with his wife,' Gramps says. 'Though he knows his animals and fish. I'll give him that.'

Gramps starts telling me the old lighthouse buildings are on sale again. He knows Joe and I used to imagine living there, when we were little. I wanted a bedroom in the round stone tower, with a circular bed and curving shelves and table and cupboards. Joe would have the room right at the top. The buildings have been derelict for years.

Evie's in the background, chipping in, and then telling him I'm paying for the phone call and not to talk for too long.

When I put the phone down, I feel slightly sad. They are getting older, Evie and Gramps; I can hear it in their voices, especially Gramps'. It comes over me in a rush that they won't be around for ever. I can't bear that. Evie and Gramps have been the steady, constant loving thread through my whole life. My rock.

The photos arrive five days later. I spread them out on my table and study them. It's exciting: I'm going to use them as my starting point for a new series of drawings. Stormy skies and seas; cloudscapes; the rough textures of stone and pebble and seaweed, and the huge bulk of the whale carcass. Evie's taken a series of photos showing people trying to move the whale with ropes and tractors, and the grainy texture of a slightly blurred photo makes me think of much older photos I've seen somewhere, of a different place: Newfoundland, I think, when whales were caught for food and oil and the seas would be red with whale blood and blubber, only the photos were black-and-white, so it looked like a spillage of black ink.

I experiment more, with black-and-white images: pencil, charcoal, pen and ink. I try a collage with chopped bits of photo of the whale on the shingle beach, and thick paint. I know these pictures are good.

Powerful, Jeanette says when I show her in class on Monday morning. 'You are really getting somewhere now, Freya.'

Gabes, his foot still in plaster, carries on filling his canvases with colour and light. He frowns as he goes past my table on his way out of the studio. He doesn't stop to look at my pictures properly, and he doesn't mention them when we meet up, later.

I don't tell him I've heard from Theo, or that I'm planning to visit Oxford. I know I should, really. But he seems so preoccupied with his own things: he's doing his application for art college in London. He's not interested in my paintings. And it's not as if he's showing much interest in me, either: not anything more than as friends.

When we go for lunch together, we chat about other things.

'How's your dad's fox?' I ask. 'Is she getting better?'

'I guess so,' Gabes says. 'But she's lost her foxy spark.' He looks at me. 'You know? The fox-ness of her. She looks like a mangy pet, fed up with being in a cage.'

'Perhaps you should just let her free,' I say. 'Perhaps she'd heal quicker like that.'

'She'd die, Freya. She wouldn't be able to catch her own food or anything. That's the point.'

'Sorry for being so stupid.'

'I wasn't suggesting that.'

'No? It sounded as if you were.'

Neither of us speaks for a while.

People leave us alone; our usual crowd go and sit inside the café instead of joining us at the table outside under the awning.

'Did something happen?' Gabes asks me, eventually. 'We were starting to be good friends, and then something changed. Did I do something wrong?'

'No,' I say. I can't tell him what I'm thinking, that the thing that changed was Theo, turning up like he did.

Muddling me.

'Come for supper again,' Gabes says, generously. 'Come home with me after college on Wednesday. Dad'll give us a lift.'

I know he's making an effort to be nice. 'OK,' I say. 'Thanks.'

It's a different sort of household without Beth and the children, and with Theo away. It all feels more normal, I suppose: an ordinary family mid-week. We have sausages and baked vegetables for supper; there's no pudding. Maddie's busy with paperwork and Kit does homework at the kitchen table once supper's over; Nick falls asleep sprawled in front of the telly.

Gabes and I do the washing-up together, and then we go outside to feed the fox and to shut away Maddie's chickens.

It's already dark, and hard to make out the fox hunched in the pen. It smells rank. When we open the door to put the scraps of food inside and top up the water in the bowl, she stays cowering in the shadows at the back of the pen. Her eyes gleam in the torch-light: dark pools.

'Poor thing.' I crouch down next to the cage. 'I see what you mean. It is like the spirit has gone out of her. I still think it would be better to let her go free. Her leg must be nearly better by now. What does your dad think?'

'Six weeks, he says, for healing a break. So only another week or so, and we can release her. Not too near here, obviously, because of the chickens.'

That's our next job. We cross the vegetable garden into the orchard. In the daytime, Maddie lets the hens out to scratch and peck under the apple and plum trees. But there's no sign of any of them now.

'They've all gone up their wooden ramp into the hen-house. They do that as soon as it gets dark,' Gabes explains. He fastens the latch on the door, and then goes round the other side to lift the lid of the nesting box. The hens stir when they hear us, and make that soft crooning sound in their throats. Gabes picks out two eggs from the straw and places them in my cupped hands. They are still faintly warm.

I carry them carefully back to the kitchen and put them in the bowl with the others. We join Nick briefly in the sitting room in front of the telly. I watch the tail end of some programme about a community choir on some estate, while he and Gabes talk about what Gabes should say in his personal statement for his UCAS form.

'You got homework?' Nick asks.

Gabes shakes his head. 'I'm all up to date with my projects. Just reading and research, now.'

It strikes me how clear Gabes is; how focused on his own plans. There's nothing wrong with that; it just doesn't leave much room for someone else. I guess he never really wanted me as a *girlfriend*. And the more I think about it, the more true that begins to sound. Gabes loves having *friends*: lots of friends, not just one special one. He likes people in groups.

Maddie settles down in her favourite chair, under the lamp near the window. She pulls out sheaves of paper from a big brown envelope, and sits to read them, pen in hand. 'Page proofs,' she explains to me. 'For my new book.'

I sit down next to Gabes on the sofa.

'I'll have the plaster off on Friday,' he says. 'Then I can get the bike going again. My life will be much easier.'

I don't know what to say. It isn't going to work out, Gabes and me. I know that now. The spark, the magic, just isn't there for him. Maybe, after all, it wasn't Gabes I was *falling for* anyway. I guess it's easy enough to make a mistake like that.

We don't hold hands. We don't even kiss goodbye when it's time for me to go home.

Dad collects me from the farm for the first time. I hear him waxing lyrical about the stone roof tiles and the beams in the kitchen with Nick.

'You coming to meet my dad?' I ask Gabes.

'OK.' Moving around is still an effort with his foot in plaster, though he can rest the heel down, now. He follows me into the kitchen.

Dad smiles. 'All set, Freya?'

I nod. 'Thanks for having me,' I say to Maddie. 'And for supper and everything.'

'You're always welcome here,' Maddie says. 'You know that. We love seeing you, don't we, Nick?'

'We do.'

'Dad, this is Gabes. My friend from college.'

Gabes steps forward to shake hands.

'Pleased to meet you, Gabes. Heard lots about you,' Dad says, even though it isn't true. I haven't mentioned him once.

I steer Dad towards the door. 'See you at college, Gabes.'

Dad drives us home. 'Gorgeous house,' he says. 'All that land, too. Nice people. Had a good time?'

I nod. 'We're just friends,' I say, quickly, to stop him before he starts going on.

Fourteen

Mist curls along the river, punctuated by the dark shapes of trees on the banks. It's early morning; the train rattles along the track, the rhythm of the wheels like a pulse in my skull. I'm travelling again, and it feels good to be moving. Through the window I glimpse a fox slipping through a gap in a hedge: I think of the one at the farmhouse, now free and living its own wild life.

The girl, *Bridie*, comes vividly into my mind. Just as we go through the tunnel at Box station, I remember that website I looked at, and the list of places where other train *fatalities* have happened. It doesn't help that the train manager keeps going on about reading the safety cards, and to report anything suspicious . . .

I change trains at Didcot, find the one for Oxford. I'm going to ask Theo about Bridie this time, I decide. A pale thin sun is just visible through the mist, and by the time the train's going past the backs of houses and parks on the outskirts of the city the mist is a thin layer, the spires and towers of churches and colleges piercing through, and the sun itself breaks out as I step on to the platform.

The station car park's full of bicycles. Everyone in Oxford rides bikes, apparently. For a fleeting second, I can imagine myself here, riding up the street on my own bike, on my way to lectures.

I get my map out, and start walking towards the town centre. The road crosses the canal: I stop to look at the houseboats and barges, just like the ones along the canal at home. Theo's student house is somewhere near this canal, further along, in an area he calls Jericho, but I'm meeting him at a café in the covered market, off High Street. It's exciting to be here, but I'm shaking with nerves, too, thinking about being alone with Theo. I put Gabes out of my mind. Try to, at least.

It's still quite early, but the streets are packed: students, tourists, ordinary people shopping. Every so often I stop to peer through the small wooden doors within bigger, ancient wooden doors that open on to beautiful grassy courtyards: cool, green spaces of privileged quiet, a stark contrast to the city streets. Two worlds, so close together – *town* and *gown*, Dad called them – it's all exactly like he described.

I check my map again: nearly there. My heart's beating fast. Any minute now and I'll see Theo . . .

Saturday morning, the indoor market's busy with shoppers queuing up for old-fashioned butchers' and greengrocers' stalls, florists and shoe shops. I find the Italian café at the opposite end to where I first came in. It's got lime green walls, a black-and-white lino floor, rows of wooden tables. Families and elderly people and – well, all sorts of *normal* people are eating breakfast. What did I expect? Not this.

I push open the door and queue up to order coffee. I've already spotted Theo at a table at the back, reading a book, pretending he hasn't noticed me, or perhaps he really is totally absorbed in the story. The café stinks of frying, hot fat, but I'm hungry so I order a bacon bap and a coffee. I wait for the Polish girl to make the coffee, and take it over with me to Theo's table.

He's wearing his usual black: skinny jeans, a fine woollen jumper, leather boots. Even the book – *Anna Karenina* – has a black cover.

'I'm reading my way through the great Russians,' he explains as he puts the book away in a battered old satchel and turns his attention to me. 'So. Freya.'

'Hello.'

He smooths his too-long fringe from his face and stares at me intently. 'You look –' he hesitates, choosing his words too carefully – 'very healthy and wholesome.'

It's not a compliment, I know that, but I'm in too good a mood to take offence. 'How are you?' I ask. 'Not at all wholesome, by the look of you.'

'Fine. Better for having two espressos. Bit of a night.'

He's being his worst, pretentious self, but I don't take much notice. I sip my coffee. The waitress brings over my bacon bap; I squeeze tomato ketchup over the bacon and eat slowly, enjoying every mouthful, just to make a point. 'Where shall we go after coffee? You said you wanted to take me somewhere?'

'When you've finished stuffing your face, I'll show you.' He smiles, despite himself.

'Want some?' I say through an extra big mouthful.

He shakes his head.

A load of students come in and order full English fry-ups at the counter. This place must be trendy in an *ironic* way, I guess. Posh kids pretending to be working class. In my mind, I'm framing images. Shame I haven't brought a camera.

'Ready then?' Theo pushes his chair back and stands up. He picks up his bag.

I'm not, really, but he clearly wants to leave. I drink my last bit of coffee and put my coat back on.

He leads the way out of the market through a different exit, into a narrow cobbled street. He unlocks his bike. 'This way.'

I walk with him beside the bike, along a series of narrow streets between high stone walls, past college entrances and more parked bikes, across a broad street at the traffic lights, down another, wider street to the Natural History Museum. He locks up the bike.

'Is this it?'

'Not quite.' He leads the way into the museum entrance, then down one of the aisles, past rows of stuffed animals and skeletons: a reindeer, a horse. He takes me to the back of the museum to some steps leading down into semi-darkness. 'The Pitt Rivers collection,' he says. 'Random objects from all over the world: *anthropological artefacts*. All a bit weird, and very wonderful. You'll love it.'

Weird is an understatement. Maybe it's the semi-darkness, or maybe the strange objects in the display cases, but I start feeling distinctly weird too. I spend ages looking at the 'animals depicted in art' collection. I get my notebook out of my bag and sketch a little Egyptian cat, and then a large gold bee, about the size of my stretched hand. I copy down the words on its handwritten label: *Gilt Bee, Burma, Mandalay. Carved and gilded wood from King Thibaw's throne.*

'My Gramps would love this,' I tell Theo.

'Yes?'

'He keeps bees. He'd like to think they were decorating a throne. Bees are really important, you know. And they are disappearing. No one knows exactly why. And if all the honeybees disappear, then humans won't be long after. We can't survive as a species without them, because of pollination – all the plants we depend on. We're all interlinked.'

'Darwin.'

'Well, yes, but it was Einstein who said the stuff about bees.'

'Can I see your drawing?'

I hand my notebook to Theo.

He studies the bee and the cat. 'They're good!'

'Don't sound so surprised!'

'It's just that Gabes' stuff never looks like anything.'

'That's because it's not meant to, silly! It's abstract art.'

Theo hands back the notebook. 'So, what time's your meeting?'

'The open day goes on till four. Some time this afternoon will be fine.'

'Want to see the shrunken heads?'

I'm not sure I do, but he shows me anyway, the glass case with the horrible heads: tiny, doll-sized, only they are human skin and real hair, with the brain taken out. There are some examples of scalps, too, where the top of someone's head has been sliced off. It makes me feel sick. The pressure building in my own head is getting worse. I turn away.

In another glass case, I find two little figures made out of moss and bark, a man and a woman. They're carved from wood and covered in moss, with hair and beard made of plant material – lichen, perhaps, with hats of bark. They are much friendlier than the heads and masks.

'Come and see these moss people, Theo. They're from Russia. To worship a god who guarded the forests.'

But Theo is still in the thrall of the shrunken heads. I can't tell what he is thinking, and he doesn't offer to tell me.

I give up and leave him there. I walk past the display of old wooden skates and snowshoes made of bone and ivory, and find my way to the exit. I'm still feeling weird. It's a relief to get outside into sunshine.

I'm not sure how long I've been there before my mobile rings.

'Hi, Theo.'

'Where the hell are you?'

'I'm outside, at the front of the building, on the steps. It's too creepy in there. I thought I was going to be sick.'

'Wait there, then. I'll come and find you.'

It seems a long time before he comes through the door. He sits beside me on the stone step. I shiver.

'We might as well go to my house, now,' he says. 'It's not far from here.'

'But what about my open day?'

'It won't matter if you don't go. It's not as if you had a definite appointment or anything, is it? No one will know.'

'Suppose not.'

'They're rubbish anyway, those sort of days. You can't tell anything about what the course is really like. It's just a huge PR exercise.'

I never really wanted to go that much in the first place. It was just an excuse for coming to Oxford. But I don't tell Theo that, of course. I'll have to think what to say to Dad, though, later.

I stand up, button up my coat and wrap my scarf round.

He's already unlocked his bike, and is wheeling it across the grass to the road. I have to run to catch up.

The roads look more ordinary, this end of town. The grand buildings give way to brick terraced houses and small shops: an Indian grocer's, a second-hand furniture shop. Theo wheels his bike expertly with one hand on the saddle, and the other touches my back lightly, as if he's steering me, too. But I'm feeling fine, now. I just needed fresh air.

'This is it.'

We stop at a brick building set at an angle to the street with a small scruffy yard at the front, a full dustbin, a row of empty bottles. The house has been divided into two: one half is smart, with neat window boxes and net curtains, and the other, with its crumpled, half-drawn blue curtain and scuffed wooden door, is evidently his.

'Who else lives here?'

'Just me and Duncan,' Theo says as he lets us in. 'Music student. Composer, conductor, all round brilliant bloke. Makes excellent curry.'

There's no sign of him, just the piano taking up a huge part of the sitting room, and through the doorway, a pile of dirty saucepans in the kitchen sink. The carpet is covered in books, paper, stuff. I follow Theo through to the kitchen at the back – there's only the two rooms downstairs – and he opens big glass doors to show me their back garden. It's almost filled with a chestnut tree, much too big for such a small garden. A few pots containing the straggling dried-up remains of tomato vines are lined along one edge of the tiny square patch of grass.

'Like it?'

'Yes. Very nice.'

'We actually grew things, last term,' Theo says. 'And cooked them.'

It's hardly a surprise, given his family, but Theo seems oddly proud of himself. 'I'll get you a rug, to sit on,' he says. 'Do you want a drink?'

'Just tea, please.'

'Hmm.' He steps back into the kitchen and rummages in the fridge. 'No milk. No fresh-enough milk, that is.'

'Black tea, then.'

He passes me a blanket and a cushion from the sitting room.

I settle myself down on the grass in the thin sunshine. It's just about warm enough, with a coat on.

Theo brings out the tea, and a cake, on a chipped white plate. 'In your honour. My special lemon and almond cake. Made with polenta instead of flour.'

'What's polenta?'

'Maize meal. Like you get everywhere in Italy.'

'Really? Never been.' I take a small bite. 'It's not bad, considering,' I say.

'Considering what?'

'You made it. And that it's made with maize meal!'

Theo laughs, and he leans in towards me, and before I really know what's happening he kisses me. On the lips: fleeting and tantalising.

My face burns. I'm suddenly aware that I'm totally alone here with Theo; no one else knows where I am. Gabes' face flashes into my mind. I push the image away again.

'You look so funny sitting there all wrapped up in your big coat,' Theo says. 'A little hungry waif.'

'You said I was *wholesome* and *healthy* before,' I say. 'What happened?'

'Dark magic in the museum, of course!' Theo says.

'Those hungry spirits, just waiting for a healthy girl like you to come along, to give them a home.'

'Don't. Not even as a joke.' I shiver again.

'What a sensitive flower you are. I'd never have expected it.'

'Why not?'

'Didn't think of you like that. You are so cheerful and positive all the time. All that swimming and cycling and outdoor stuff you do.'

'Only you could make that sound insulting,' I say. 'Anyway, you can talk! You swim and cycle too.'

'But I'm not relentlessly cheerful, or quite so positive.'

I don't like him saying that.

'And now I've offended you.'

'Yes.'

Theo frowns.

'There's nothing wrong with being cheerful. It's better than being moody and pretentious and arrogant!' I say.

Theo cuts another slab of cake for himself and eats it slowly. He looks at me from under that stupid fringe and makes his mouth go into a sort of pout, a caricature of someone who's sorry.

I can't seem to stop myself. 'You're not the only person who reads poetry and long, complicated novels and has deep thoughts and . . . and sad things have happened to them.'

Theo looks genuinely hurt.

I'm glad.

Finally he apologises. 'I'm sorry I upset you,' Theo

says. 'I really didn't mean to. I like you a lot, Freya. Always have done, from the beginning. I was just being – I don't know – glib? It's just how I talk. A habit. Covering up what I'm really feeling.'

For a second I catch a clear glimpse of a different Theo. Someone much more vulnerable than he lets on. Someone I could really like.

I change the subject. 'Your cake is delicious, actually,' I say. 'And I love your house.'

'Shall I show you round?'

'Yes please.'

It's really tiny; just two two bedrooms and a small bathroom upstairs. Theo's room is at the back, above the kitchen, looking over the garden. The tree fills the window space, throwing deep shadows into the room.

Theo turns on the desk light. He has lined up rows of photographs along a bookshelf, almost an echo of the photo display on the piano back at Home Farm. The familiar faces of his family smile out at me. And there's one more face: the one I've been half expecting to see: the girl he played with as a child, and was fascinated by as a teenager, and who has planted herself in my brain, too: a ghost girl.

In his photo she's older, with long dark hair, thin face, dark eyes; she's wearing a sleeveless cotton dress. Her arms are painfully thin.

'That's Bridie, isn't it?' I ask.

Theo's sitting cross-legged on the bed. He doesn't look at me. 'Yes.'

I pull out a chair, to sit facing him. I notice, now, how obsessively tidy the room is compared to downstairs. The books and DVDs are shelved alphabetically; his guitar hangs by its strap on a special hook, his clothes (almost all black) hang neatly on a rail. Even the floor looks clean.

'And?' Theo says.

'Gabes told me about her.'

'I know.'

'You do?'

'Yes, of course. We're brothers. Closer than you think.'

'So you know about . . . me, on the train, at the funeral and everything?'

'Yes.' He looks so terribly sad.

'You weren't there, were you?'

'No. I hate funerals. I couldn't bear it.'

I watch his face.

'I think about her all the time,' Theo says. 'I go over in my mind what I could have said or done, to stop her. But I had no idea . . . I mean, I knew she got depressed, that she was ill, but . . . well, there was so much I didn't know about her. Mum told me, afterwards, about the drugs, and what was happening in her brain . . . Mum felt guilty too, for not saving her.'

'We felt like that when my brother died,' I say. 'My parents, Gramps and Evie, me.'

'But it was an accident, right?'

'Yes. I know that, now. But I didn't always. For a while I wondered whether it was on purpose . . . that he meant to die.' The memory of that summer is still so sharp and powerful I have to steel myself not to weep buckets all over again.

I concentrate on Theo. 'What was Bridie like when you were both little?'

Theo stays silent for a while. He looks up at me. 'She was funny and odd and very, very naughty.' He leans back against the wall next to the bed, half smiles. 'She always pushed things to the limit. Like, there was this game we played where you had to jump off the stairs on to the hall floor, and you had to keep going higher, to see how many steps you could jump off and she'd keep going, four, five, six stairs – crazy, she almost broke her neck doing that. Climbing up trees, she'd always have to go way too high, crawl out along stupidly thin branches at the top. Her favourite thing was dares. Taking it in turn to dare each other to do something – silly, dangerous things, mostly.'

'Gabes told me she pushed Kit out of the window.'

'She didn't actually push him. Mum got there in time. Maybe Bridie wouldn't have actually done it for real. It was a game.'

'Not a very nice one. Not for Kit. Or your mum!'

'No. She wasn't *nice*. You wouldn't ever use that word for Bridie.'

'What word would you use?'

'Exciting? Scary? I don't know. Never boring. You felt like you were alive, being with her, because she made you feel everything so intensely.'

The irony of that sinks in. *Alive*.

Theo looks at me again. 'You know something? That kind of compulsion to take risks . . . I've met other people like that here, in Oxford. These medical students I was friends with last year, they were like that: adrenaline junkies. Climbing, caving, hang-gliding, drinking too much . . . I reckon those are just more expensive, grown-up ways of making yourself feel you're alive. In the daytime they had to do all this horrible stuff to do with illness and bodies and death, so in the evening and at weekends they pushed out the boundaries of living.'

'It's an interesting theory,' I say. 'It sort of makes sense. But why would Bridie . . . what was going on for her?'

Theo shrugs. 'Who knows? Something very dark and damaged. Mum says she wanted attention, wanted to make sure people noticed her, needed to convince herself and the world that she existed.'

Theo looks gloomier than ever. 'But she glittered and sparkled, too. A bit manic, maybe, but at the time she . . . well, she was beautiful to me. Painfully thin. Like glass. Of course she'd break.'

'I'm sorry,' I say. 'It hurts you to talk about her.'

'It's not the talking that actually hurts though, is it? The hurt's happened already. And mine means nothing, compared to hers.'

I rack my brains to remember the comforting things people have said to me, over the last three years. 'Sad and terrible things happen. It's how you react to them that makes the difference.'

'What do you mean?'

'What you *do*, after. I think that's why I *so* want to make my life matter, to live a good life: because Joe didn't have the chance. I don't want to be bitter and sad and hopeless.'

Theo gives me the saddest smile. 'You know what, Freya? The truth is, you are *so* the least bitter, sad person I know. And you've already made a difference to me.'

I shiver. There's something really scary about him saying that. It's as if Theo's words tie me to him in some way. Like there's a new kind of pact between us. As if I've got to go on making a difference to him. Or else what?

What might he do?

The front door opens. We hear Duncan come in and go into the kitchen. The floor's so thin we can even hear the sound of him flicking the switch on the kettle.

Theo gets up and smooths the bed covers where they were creased up under him. 'In a minute I'll introduce you to the lovely Duncan, but you must promise not to fall in love with him. Of course he'll fall in love with you, though. How could he not?'

'Meaning what?'

'You are the bright star come to dwell amongst us. Our muse and our salvation. He'll be writing songs for you before you know it.'

'You talk such utterly pretentious rubbish, Theo Fielding!' I shove him back on the bed, and he pulls me down with him, and we kiss.

Properly, this time. Not the quick touch of lips like earlier, in the garden, but deep and dark and dangerous and delicious. I have that sensation of *falling* . . .

out of control . . . all over again. I know it's a mistake: he's five years older than me; he's *Theo*, for God's sake! Gabes' brother. Mixed-up, contradictory, crazy Theo!

I know.

I know.

I know.

Fifteen

My train leaves at quarter to six. It's a mad scramble to get to the station on time.

'Why don't you stay?' Theo asks, as I pick up my coat. 'Or at least get a later train?'

'I can only use my ticket on this one. I know, boring. But I don't have any money.'

'I'll pay.'

'No. Thank you. But no.'

Duncan comes to the door to wave me off. 'See you again soon. It was a total pleasure to meet you!' He blows me a kiss.

'Thanks for tea and everything,' I say.

'Wait a second!' Theo says. 'I want to get you something.' He runs upstairs.

Duncan smiles at me. 'He's happier already,' he tells me. 'Well done, Freya!'

'I haven't done anything!'

'No? The evidence is to the contrary!'

Theo thumps back down the stairs holding a see-through plastic folder with sheets of typed paper inside. 'Reading matter, for your journey home.' He shoves the folder into my bag.

I don't ask what it is. Poems, I guess, and my heart sinks, ever so slightly.

We run through the streets of Jericho, past St Barnabas Church, along Walton Street and then turn right into Worcester Street. It's already dusk; cars are streaming out of the city centre, lights reflecting off the wet road. At some point in the late afternoon it must have rained.

We arrive on the platform just as the train slides in. I lean from the train doorway to kiss him goodbye. 'Send me another postcard, when you have time. Thanks for a lovely time!'

I settle myself in my seat, still smiling. I don't look back, out of the window. The train gathers speed, rushing into the darkness, taking me home.

It's not till I've changed trains at Didcot that I get out the folder of paper he put in my bag. I leaf through the pages. Not poems, but some sort of story, typed on thin white paper. I start to read.

It doesn't take me long to realise that the story is about Bridie, and that's why he wanted me to read it. It's about him too, I guess, even though the boy in the story isn't called Theo. What I *don't* know, and can't tell, is how much is real, how much is made up – Theo's fantasy about her.

In the story, it's the morning of Bridie's eighteenth birthday, and the boy has made her a cake. That bit I can believe. He's bought birthday candles specially: pastel colours good enough to eat: candy pink and lemon yellow and pale blue and soft lime. The story starts as he's walking down this street past a row of derelict houses, quite close to the railway. When he arrives at the squat where she's living, he sees her at the window, her face like *a pale flower*.

She runs down the stairs and comes to the door, but she won't let him in.

'We're going out,' she tells him.

'Where?'

'I'll show you. Follow me.'

She takes him to this rusting old blue Ford estate car: she says she's borrowed it from one of the guys in the squat (later, the boy wonders if she stole it). She is going to drive them to the seaside. Has she got a driving licence? No, course not. But she's picked up the basics of driving, more or less, from all the times she's been in the car with this other guy. And they go, the car doing those rabbit hops as she starts off, until she gets the gears right. After that, it's fine.

That can't be true. Can it?

In Theo's story, anyway, she makes the boy read the map and the road signs and somehow they make it to the Gower coast – that's way beyond Swansea, in west Wales: it's motorway all the way once you've got on the M4, and then some wiggling about beyond Swansea on small roads and they get lost loads but they are laughing and singing and having fun and finally they get to the beach Bridie has remembered from when she was a little girl and visited with her mum.

There's a huge expanse of sand, and a river flowing right across it, and stepping stones to cross at low tide, but at high tide the whole beach will be covered and Bridie wants to wait till that happens, to see the river filling up and the water submerging everything, and she wants to sleep the night in a cave, and swim in moonlight . . .

It's too windy to light the candles on the beach, so they climb up the cliff and find a cave, and the boy sings 'Happy Birthday', and Bridie blows out the candles, and they make a camp, and collect driftwood for a fire, and stay all night, while the tide comes in and washes over the beach . . .

The sound of the sea lashing the cliffs fills their heads all night, and there's no way they can swim with the water so high there's no beach left. They watch the sky clear, and it's filled with bright stars, and the moonlight shines on Bridie's face, making it white and strange, like the face of a ghost.

In Theo's story, Bridie is so vividly alive it takes my breath away. I can see the beach and the cliff and the night sky as clearly as if I've been there. It's almost a shock to find I'm still on the train, travelling westwards. When I peer out of the window, my own face reflects back at me, pale and troubled. I fold the pages back into my bag, and my hands are shaking.

Sixteen

Now, safely back home in my room, I don't know what to make of it all. Oxford, Theo, Bridie. I put the story safely away in a drawer, change my clothes, go downstairs for supper.

'Black bean chilli with avocado salsa,' Mum announces proudly, placing the steaming dish on the kitchen table. 'Thought I'd try something a bit different for a change.'

It's a shame that I'm not hungry, really. I pick at the salsa and some rice.

Dad shovels the chilli beef into his mouth and fires off questions about the Oxford Art course. 'What did they say about the lecturers? Did you meet any? See their work? You want to be somewhere where they are all actively painting. And do they actually teach the basics? Drawing?'

I sigh. I don't want to have to lie, so I don't say anything.

Mum glances at me. She knows something's up. 'Freya's tired, Martin! Let her eat in peace. Let's talk about something else, for now.'

So they have a conversation about the garden, and Mum starts talking about what we should do for Christmas this year. It's become this huge issue, ever since Joe died. How to spend the least painful day together.

'We should have your parents over,' Mum says to Dad. 'We could pay for their flights, this once.'

'Or we could go there.'

Mum shakes her head. 'No. I don't think so. I don't think that's a very good idea at all.'

'Why make such a big thing about it?' I say. 'It's just a day.'

They both look at me, and then at each other.

I pick up my plate and take it over to the dishwasher. 'I'm going upstairs.'

Up in my room, I text Miranda. **Are you free tomorrow? Can we do something FUN?**

It's ages before she replies. I've almost given up; have had a bath and got into bed. I try reading, but my mind keeps drifting away from the page. At last my phone bleeps. Text message.

Ice-skating? Meet 11am station? Unless yr mum/dad can give lift?

Yes! 11 at station x I text straight back, and then I turn off the light and burrow under the duvet, as if the soft darkness will keep my own thoughts at bay.

It's the most fun we've had together since . . . I don't know, Miranda's last birthday party, probably. She's much better at skating than I am; she used to have lessons, after school, and she can do all the stuff like turns and going backwards and even a bit of ice dancing. It's packed with people, being Sunday morning, but mostly families, younger kids. We lace up our boots and then hobble over to the rink, and holding hands, to begin with, while I get my confidence up, we skate round the edge of the ice near enough for me to grab the side rail if I start to tumble. After a few goes, I've got my balance right and we go faster, further from the edge. The effortless speed is exhilarating! We let go of our hands, and Miranda shows off her pirouettes and jumps and figures of eight. She teaches me how to go backwards, how to stop quickly, how to turn. We laugh and laugh, and then I make a mistake, and trip up and land hard on my bottom on the ice, and we laugh even more.

We come off the ice for a drink at the funny old-fashioned café at the side. Our cheeks are glowing, I'm wet through, but I feel brilliant. We sip milk-shakes through straws. It's like being ten again, when it was so much easier to just have fun and not worry about anything.

'So,' Miranda says, doing an extra-loud slurp through the straw to get up the last chocolatey bubbles. 'What happened yesterday?'

She knows me so well!

'I didn't go to the open day thing at all.'

'Ah.'

'I met Theo, instead.'

'Theo?'

'Gabes' brother.'

'Freya!'

'Don't be shocked!'

'But I am! What were you thinking of? Are you completely crazy?'

'Don't say that. I know, it's stupid. He's too old. He's Gabes' brother. But I had such a lovely time. We met in a café. He took me to this extraordinary museum. We went back to his house. We talked and talked. He kissed me.'

Miranda looks stricken. She doesn't speak at first. Then she says, 'That's bad. Very bad. And worse than you think.'

'What do you mean?'

'Well, I didn't know anything about Theo, did I? And I didn't realise you hadn't told Gabes about you going to Oxford, obviously, since you didn't tell me you hadn't. Why would I guess a thing like that? So when I bumped into Gabes in town, yesterday, I just mentioned about you being in Oxford for the day, and I suppose he did look a bit peculiar, but I didn't know why, then . . . Now it makes more sense.' She pushes the empty glass round with her finger. She looks back at me. 'What I don't get, more than anything, Freya, is why you have kept all this secret from me. I thought we were best friends.'

'We are,' I say. 'I'm so sorry, I know it seems weird, the whole thing.'

'You planned it all out, and you didn't tell me.'

'I know.' My voice sounds feeble, pathetic.

'You didn't tell me because I'd have made you see what a mistake it was. I'd have stopped you. Honestly, you are totally hopeless, Freya.'

A little spurt of fire rises up inside me. 'You don't understand. It's not like you think. Gabes and I aren't going out together. We're just friends. That's all.'

'Really? Does he know that? And you're not going to be *friends* any more, I don't think. Not when he finds out about you and Theo.'

'You won't tell him.'

'No. But you should.'

I unwrap a chocolate bar and break off half for Miranda. Is she right? Is it anybody's business, any of it, other than Theo's and mine? I know the answer, really. I sigh deeply. Why do things get so complicated? I wish Miranda and I really were just ten years old, ice-skating, scoffing chocolate, best friends for ever and ever.

'Remember that rhyme, from primary school?' I say. '*Make friends, make friends, never, never break friends.*'

She scowls at me. 'And?'

'Nothing; it just came into my head. Things were easier then.'

'Well. Yes. Duh! We were kids. And now we've growed up, remember? No one said it would be easy.'

'Grown, not growed.'

'You!' Miranda stands up and pushes me, and I shove her back, and we start laughing again. 'Come on, let's get moving!' She grabs my arm and we hobble back to the ice, and soon we're gliding smoothly off again, arm in arm. We leave our differences behind. We cross our arms in front, still holding hands, and then twist, turn, arms behind us, like an elaborate dance movement. The feeling of speed, of lightness, feet gliding over ice, through air, spins a new mood over us both.

The music changes. An announcement about *anyone with a blue band* comes over the loudspeakers. Our two-hour slot is up.

We're tired out. We sit for ages, unlacing our boots, collecting our shoes, sorting out coats, talking all the while about this and that; nothing important, nothing that will spoil things between us.

We emerge from the skating rink into a wet afternoon. We walk slowly back to the station and wait for a train home. 'We should go skating again, with the college crowd,' Miranda says. 'We all need more fun in our lives!'

'You are so right. Let's go next weekend.'

'You're not going back to Oxford, then?'

'No. Nothing planned.'

'Tell me, next time?'

'Yes.'

'Promise?'

'Cross my heart. Hope to die if I tell a lie!'

We both laugh.

I give her a hug. 'Thanks, Miranda!'

'Whatever for?'

'Being you. Being here. Understanding me.'

So it's so much worse, that I break my promise.

I don't tell Gabes about me and Theo, even when I go over to his house to see the newborn kittens.

I don't tell Miranda that Theo phones, twice. Sends me a postcard. Invites me for another weekend.

Seventeen

It's a bitterly cold day in early December. Because the Oxford University term is so short, theirs has already finished, whereas we've got another three weeks left at college.

Theo's waiting for me at the station. As the train pulls in, I can already see him scanning the carriages ahead, and then he spots me and our eyes meet. A delicious shiver runs down my spine.

He waits for me to open the door, his face solemn. He's got his coat collar turned up, and a black hat and grey scarf. His hands are pale and naked-looking.

I step down on to the platform. He holds both my hands in his for a second.

'You're freezing!' I say. 'Sorry to be so late. There were wrong signals or something. We waited for ages outside Didcot.'

He shakes his head.

I know I sound utterly banal. I can hear my own voice, babbling rubbish as we cross the car park.

We pause for him to unlock his bike, and then he

pushes it along beside us as we walk back towards the city. We stop on the bridge to stare down at the frozen canal from the bridge. The houseboats are all marooned in ice.

'*Steadily going nowhere! Happy the whole day long!*' The silly line from an advert on telly pops into my head and out of my mouth without warning. The more I want to be intelligent and mature, the worse I get. I put my arm through his, anyway, and we push on forward into the crowded streets.

'Coffee first?' Theo asks.

'Yes! Can we go somewhere else, this time? Not that greasy spoon place.'

Theo shrugs but he steers me down a narrow alleyway and along a cobbled street to a different café. He locks the bike outside and we go in and sit at the window table. We order coffee, and toasted crumpets because we're both suddenly starving. It seems the right sort of food for Oxford.

Theo warms his hands under his armpits, hugging himself. Now he's taken off his coat he looks thin, much thinner than last time I saw him. His face is pale, his eyes too dark.

'How's the term been?' I ask him.

'Mad. Too much work. Too many essays, all due in the same date.'

'But you've finished, now?'

'Yes.' He narrows his eyes as he looks at me. 'Did you read the story? The one I wrote, I mean.'

'Yes.'

'You didn't mention it.'

'No. I didn't know what to say.'

'Did you like it?'

'Yes. But it made me confused. Like, was it made up? Or real?'

'Does it matter?'

'To me, yes.'

He leans across the table so his face is close to mine. 'What did you think, though, as you read it? That it happened like that? Could have happened?'

He frightens me when he's this intense.

I think, fast.

'Yes,' I say. 'It was totally believable. The girl – Bridie – seemed so real and alive it made me really sad . . .' my voice fades out. 'That she . . . that she isn't, any more.'

Theo doesn't speak for a while. Our coffees arrive, and we eat the crumpets: two each, with butter dripping through the holes and pooling on to the plate.

'But she lives on, in a way, through my story, doesn't she?' Theo says.

'Yes, I guess . . .'

'And I might write more about her.'

I don't know what to say to that. Bridie's ghost is hovering between us now, an unwelcome guest at the table.

'I hear her voice, sometimes,' Theo says.

I look up at him. 'Yes?' My heart beats faster. 'That happened to me, too, after Joe died. I'd hear his voice, just as I was dropping off to sleep. I'd even see him, sometimes, or feel his arm brush mine . . . it's natural, when you've loved someone, Theo.'

'No, not like that. I actually hear her. She talks to me,' Theo says.

I don't try and argue. There's no point.

I try to put it out of my head, but it's as if a shadow has fallen over us. Everything has shifted for a second. Things are not quite as they should be.

'So,' I say brightly, to lift my own spirits. 'Can we go to the Botanical Gardens, next? They'll be amazing in the frost.'

Theo makes an effort to lift the mood too. 'You can draw them. Did you bring your notebook?'

'Of course! But it's too cold to sit still and draw,' I say. 'I'd like to see the river. And I want to find the seat where Lyra and Will sat, at the end of the last *His Dark Materials* book.'

'See, you muddle up real life and stories all the time, too,' Theo says.

We put on our coats and scarves and Theo pays. 'Ready?'

I nod.

'There's a place on the river where people swim, all year round,' Theo says. 'Even in the winter.'

'Well, that's just crazy!'

'I thought you liked river swimming?'

I know we're both remembering being at the stream together at Home Farm. The time we first met.

I'm thinking about what he said, on the way back from our swim that late summer afternoon: *I wish I'd found you first.*

'What's your friend Duncan doing today?' I say.

'Why?' Theo stops and for a second he looks almost

angry. 'He's packing up, if you must know, ready to go home to Birmingham.'

'There's no need to be so spiky! I only asked.'

Theo recovers himself. 'Sorry, Freya. I don't know what's the matter with me.'

We go past the big bookshop.

Theo points to a book in the window display, about *finding your inner fish*.

I laugh.

The tension between us gradually begins to ease.

The Botanical Gardens are thick with frost. It has edged the leaves with white fur, transformed seed heads into white baubles; the grass is like cake icing, crunchy under our boots. We run over the lawns, making maze patterns for each other to trace round and round. Our breath makes clouds in the still air.

It's much too cold to sit for long on the bench where Lyra and Will sat in the story. We walk along next to the river for a while, and then we go into the glass-houses, where the air is warmer, before we start walking back a different way, skirting through the backs of the colleges.

We're both freezing. The sun still hasn't come out, but the frosty air turns to a grey mistiness, damp that seeps through clothing. We stop off to buy food at the covered market off High Street. I buy a postcard to send to Evie and Gramps, and another, for Danny. But that makes me feel bad, somehow. Because I'm here with Theo, and I know they wouldn't approve . . .

On an impulse, Theo grabs my arm and takes me

down a narrow medieval street and through one of those secret wooden doors into a small courtyard.

'Are we allowed?' I whisper.

'It's fine,' Theo says. 'I want you to see what it's like, inside.'

We go through another door, across a small courtyard with a beautiful plane tree in the centre. From a lit window two storeys up the first notes of music drift across the courtyard as someone begins to practise the piano. It's all quite magical. We go up some steps, and through a door, and I find myself in a chapel, the light coming through a huge medieval stained-glass window at one end. The wooden ceiling is decorated with paintings of angels, and a real boy is sitting on a chair, playing a lute. We might have stepped back hundreds of years.

We stand together at the entrance to the nave, and turn to look up at the tower above, just as the bell begins to strike. A crowd of tourists comes through the door. Someone begins to explain the history of the chapel. We tiptoe out again, back through the way we came, out on to the street.

We don't say much. We weave our way back to Jericho. My feet are tired. I'm cold and damp. It's a relief to finally arrive at Theo's house.

Duncan's already gone. He's left a note for Theo on the kitchen table, with a P.S. for me. Theo hands over the piece of paper. It's an invitation to us both for a New Year's Eve Party, at his home in Birmingham. 'What do you think?' Theo asks.

'No way will my parents let me go,' I say. 'Not so far, just for a party, and with people they don't know.'

‘So, how come they didn’t mind you coming to Oxford to see me?’

I feel myself blush. ‘I didn’t tell them.’

‘So where do they think you are?’

‘I said I’d been invited to Home Farm, again. That I’d stay in Laura’s room, like I did before. It seemed easier, somehow, because . . . well, now my dad’s been there and met your parents . . .’ I’m so embarrassed I stumble over my words.

Theo stares at me.

Is he shocked that I lied?

It was too horribly easy to lie to Mum and Dad. They trust me, I guess. I’ve never given them reason not to.

‘So they think right now you are with Gabes?’ Theo says.

I don’t answer, and Theo doesn’t say anything either.

I stare at the scrap of paper in my hand, at Duncan’s flamboyant handwriting in black ink. I look at our two names written side by side: *Freya and Theo*, as if we are a couple. Is that what Duncan thinks? What has Theo said about me, exactly?

Now Duncan’s gone home for the holidays, Theo and I are going to be alone together in the house for a whole weekend. No one knows I am here. It’s beginning to feel a bit scary.

Nothing will happen unless I want it to, I tell myself. And my instincts all say, *Wait, go slowly, don’t rush into anything!*

* * *

We make a meal together with the food we bought at the market. Theo, like everyone in his family, knows how to cook. I help chop onions and slice mushrooms and carrots. While the beef casserole is slowly cooking in the oven, he shows me how to make a cake he calls Linzertorte, with hazelnuts and cocoa and cherry jam. The kitchen is warm and steamy, scented with allspice and nutmeg. It begins to feel more normal, making a meal together; not so intense.

'Do you see Beth, sometimes?' I ask Theo. 'She lives in Oxford, doesn't she?'

'Summertown,' Theo says. 'North of here. I've been there once this term. Mostly, at the weekends when I've got more free time, she's staying at Home Farm. As you know.'

I think guiltily of my last visit there, with Gabes, to see the kittens just after they were born. Four tiny tabby-and-white kittens, small as mice. It was mid-week, so Beth wasn't around. We weren't there for long, and after supper and kitten-viewing we went back to town for a film with Miranda and some of Gabes' friends. And I felt terrible the whole time, because I didn't say anything to Gabes about Theo, and he didn't say anything either, about Miranda telling him I'd been to Oxford . . . and it was a relief that we were hardly alone at all the whole evening.

Theo's phone rings, and he goes through to the sitting room to talk. I listen, of course, but he doesn't give much away. It sounds as if he's arranging for us to meet some people later on. Or possibly for them to come here. I'm slightly nervous. They will all be much older than me. Twenty, twenty-one. University students.

I look up as he comes into the kitchen.

'All right?' he asks.

I nod.

'Want a drink?'

'Just tea, please.'

'I bought some milk this time, specially for you.' He opens the fridge and gets out a carton. 'See?' He plonks a tea bag into an orange-and-white-striped mug with the words *Brave New World* in black letters on one side.

'Have you read the book?' I ask him.

'Huxley? Yes. The title's a quotation, from Shakespeare,' Theo says.

'*How beauteous mankind is! O brave new world that has such people in it.* It's from *The Tempest*. I know because it's Gramps' favourite play.' I feel rather proud of myself, but Theo doesn't look particularly impressed. He starts to wash up the load of pans and bowls we've used. I take my tea into the sitting room and try to make myself cosy on the sofa. I draw my knees up under the blue blanket someone's left in a heap.

'Do you want to light a fire?' Theo calls. 'There's wood and stuff in the basket.'

I kneel on the rug in front of the fireplace, and make a wigwam of the smallest bits of wood, and scrunch up newspaper, light it with a match. The thin blue flame licks along the edge of the paper, flares up as it catches the dry sticks. I add more wood, piece by piece, the way Evie's taught me. It's odd, the way I keep thinking about her and Gramps. It's the third time today.

I draw the curtains and pull the sofa closer to the fire, and sit with my back against it, the blanket over my knees, to wait for the room to warm up. Theo is still busy cleaning up the kitchen. The room gets quietly darker, and I don't put the lights on. It's better this way, with just the light from the fire.

Theo comes to join me. We sit very close, our bodies touching all along one side. I sip my tea, the mug warm between my hands. We stare at the fire, and neither if us says anything for a long time.

'She couldn't sit still,' Theo says. He's thinking about *her*, again. Bridie.

'Not for even a few minutes. Last time I saw her, she was all nervy and on edge, her hands twitching, even when we were sitting down. She kept getting up, and she had to be smoking, or drinking, or something, the whole time. She was so thin, it was as if her skin was transparent. I knew she was ill, really badly ill. Why didn't I do something?'

In the light from the fire I see tears on his face. A memory washes over me, of my brother biting back tears – already, aged about fifteen, ashamed to show his emotions. Thinking about Joe makes me braver with Theo.

I put my arms around him. 'It wasn't your fault. There wasn't anything you could do,' I whisper into his hair.

Izzy's light voice comes into my head, from the summer I spent with her, the year after Joe died. She made me a necklace with a pebble from the beach: *a talisman to cure you from sadness.*

Theo needs someone to help him get over his sadness, like Izzy helped me, and that someone could be me, if only I could work out exactly how. And then maybe something good can happen out of all this, and I don't need to feel bad about seeing Theo, and hurting Gabes . . .

While we wait for the dinner to cook, Theo tells me about the poet John Keats. He's been reading him this term. 'He wanted to live a life of sensation, rather than thought. You know, experience things in the moment. Feel everything.' Theo reaches over to the coffee table and picks up a small hardback book. 'Listen to this. It's about trying to catch a moment of beauty.'

I've heard the poem before; that famous one about a Greek urn.

'She cannot fade, though thou hast not thy bliss,
For ever wilt thou love, and she be fair!'

Is he still thinking about Bridie?

He flicks through the pages of the book and finds a second poem to read aloud. He reads well: the words make a kind of sense to me even though some of them are very old-fashioned. And they are beautiful: they linger in the air, casting a kind of spell over us both. We watch tiny sparks spiral up like fireflies as the logs slowly sink and crumble and turn to ash.

Theo goes to the kitchen to check the dinner. 'Won't be long,' he says.

'Good! I'm ravenous!'

Finally it's ready and we can eat.

There's a knock at the door about nine.

Theo opens it. 'Harry! Toby!'

'We're on our way to the pub,' the tall one – Harry – says. 'Coming?'

'Come in and meet Freya first,' Theo says. 'And seeing as we're about to have pudding, you can join us.'

Theo cuts the Linzertorte into slices and we eat almost all of it, piece by delicious piece, even though it's so sweet and rich. Theo seems different with his friends. I go quiet. They are all so much older and cleverer than me.

Harry goes over to the piano and plays some classical piece, mournful and lovely. I think of that moment in the college courtyard, the notes of music hanging in the cold air. They each take turns. Theo isn't as good as they are – both Harry and Toby are studying music, like Duncan – but he's a million times better than I would be. Harry and Toby play a duet.

I stay in the background, listening, but not saying much. They don't seem to mind, or even to notice.

Toby starts rolling a joint.

'I'm tired, Theo,' I say. 'I'm going up to bed.'

'Night night, Freya!' Toby says. 'Good to meet you.'

At the top of the stairs I hesitate.

I turn right, into Duncan's empty room.

Theo comes up after a while and stands in the bedroom doorway.

I'm still fully clothed, sitting on the bed in the dark.

'What's the matter? Aren't you coming with us for a drink? Or are you fed up with us? Do you *disapprove*?'

'No,' I say, though I do, a bit. 'Had you forgotten? I'm sixteen, Theo! Not old enough to drink in pubs, not legally, anyway.'

'No one's going to know,' Theo says. 'They'll assume you're our age. A student.'

I shake my head.

'Do you mind if I go?' he asks.

'No.'

'You'll be OK. I mean, it's perfectly safe round here.'

'Of course! It's fine, Theo. I'm tired, I'll go to sleep. I'll see you in the morning.'

The front door bangs shut behind them.

I lie there in the silent house. It's a bit weird of Theo, isn't it? Going off with his friends like that and leaving me here, when I've come all this way to see him.

But, surprisingly, I do sleep, deeply and without dreaming.

Next morning, I wake up to a freezing cold house. I get dressed quickly, go downstairs. Theo's coat and shoes are lying in a heap on the floor, so I know he did come back last night even though I didn't hear him. I try to get the fire going, but there's not enough wood in the basket to keep it burning for long. I pick up all the empty beer and cider bottles lying around the sitting room and put them in the bin in the kitchen. I make tea. I stand at the French windows, staring out at the small back garden. The grass is thick with frost; tiny birds flit in and out of the bare branches of the tree. The sky is clearing to brilliant blue as the sun climbs higher. I'm so cold I find my coat and put that on, an extra layer.

The house is completely silent. I pick up the volume of Keats' poems and find the second one Theo read aloud to me last night and read it again to myself. A love poem. What does *that* mean? Was Theo trying to tell me something? Or was that all about Bridie too?

While I wait for him to surface, I do a series of quick drawing exercises in my sketchbook: one minute, then five minutes, then drawing with my opposite hand, which taps into the other side of your brain, and then drawing without looking at the paper. I draw the tree. I try to draw from memory the figure of the boy playing the lute in the chapel, but I can't get it right.

I switch the radio on.

Finally, Theo appears.

I smile. 'It's so beautiful outside! Let's go out!'

He frowns. 'What, now? So early?'

'It's not so early. I've been up for hours. And yes, now: before the day spoils.'

All the murk and darkness of yesterday has cleared away in the brilliance of sunshine on frost.

'Come on! Run with me!' I tug Theo's hand, pull him along through the empty streets.

He grumbles to begin with, but after a while he gets into it.

'I know where I want to take you,' he says, and he runs faster, dragging me this time.

We are like two children, excited and silly, running and sliding on the iced puddles, watching our breath make clouds of dragon steam. We hold hands, and slide together, and laugh and laugh when we both skid over. Our voices echo down the street, bouncing off the high brick walls of the church we run past, and then muffled by the trees as we take a short cut along the shadowy edge of the frozen canal. The boats are silent. No sign of anyone else awake, even here.

We come out of the shadows into the brightness of Port Meadow. It comes as a surprise to me, this vast flat open field so close to the city where horses roam freely over the marshy grass. Everything's shiny, sparkling, reflecting light. The river looks like molten silver. The horses stop grazing, lift their heads to watch us, and then, all together, they toss their heads and run too, in a wide arc, away to the edge of the field, whinnying as they go.

I let go of Theo's hand and spread out my arms, running as fast as I can, down to the river. It's like flying, almost, with the rush of cold air on my face, freezing my ears, blowing back my hair.

I wait for Theo to catch up. He doesn't look so pale. His eyes look brighter. It's good for him to be outside like this, and running, and mucking around. He doesn't do it enough. He's too serious to play, usually. Takes *himself* too seriously.

The shallow edge where the river runs against the sandy bank has frozen into ribbons of white lace.

'Imagine,' I say to Theo as he comes close up, 'if it stayed cold long enough for the river to freeze solid! We could skate on the ice, like Hatty did.'

'Hatty?'

'You know, the girl in *Tom's Midnight Garden,* who skates on the frozen river from Castleford all the way to Ely and Tom skates with her.'

'I don't know what you are talking about!' Theo says.

'Hah! And you call yourself a reader!'

'Well, I have some things to catch up on, clearly.' Theo puts his arms round me and hugs me tight. He rests his chin on the top of my head. I breathe in the musky smell of woollen coat; *boy*.

'Shall we walk on to Binsey? Or back to town for breakfast?' Theo asks.

'Breakfast, please! Race you back to the bridge!'

We go to our café on Holywell Street and afterwards I insist we go to the Darwin exhibition. I spend ages studying his notebook drawings of the Tree of Life. At one level, it's simply an image of how everything is connected to everything else; how the whole of life comes from a single source. And it's a metaphor, too: how if you mess with one part of the natural world, it puts it all out of sync. Like the honeybees.

My mind's whizzing. If everything is interconnected, then what happens to anyone else is going to affect me. Like, what happened to Bridie . . . I have to care about it. And if I put that on a global scale, I have to face other uncomfortable truths. What happens to a street child in Brazil, or a family in Uganda or a teenager in Afghanistan . . . it all matters. I can't stick my head in the sand and think it doesn't concern me. After a while, my head begins to spin. I try to explain what I'm thinking to Theo.

He shakes his head. 'That way madness lies,' he says. 'If you are going to take on the suffering of the universe, Freya, you will go crazy. It's too much to feel. Impossible. Overwhelming.'

And yet I don't feel like that. Not negative, or depressed. Quite the opposite: I feel life zinging along every nerve. I'm awake, alert, as if my eyes have opened to something so blindingly obvious I don't know why everyone can't see it.

'If we're all connected,' I tell Theo, 'we're not just connected to the sad things that happen, but all the wonder and the beauty and the goodness, too! And there's so much more of the good and beautiful things.'

'When will you be coming back home?' I ask Theo at the station when it's time for me to go back.

'Next week, or the one after.'

'Will you all be at Home Farm for Christmas?'

'Of course! You should come, too.'

'Really? Could I? I'd love that so much!'

What about Gabes? I push the thought away again.

I can so easily imagine how different their family Christmas will be from mine. There would be loads of people, a huge delicious meal, talking and arguing and laughter. Fun. Whereas in our house, there will be my parents' quiet, unspoken sadness, where every tiny thing reminds them how much they are missing Joe.

It's not that I don't miss him too; I do. But I've got my own life now, here, and stretching ahead, and I refuse to spend every minute feeling sad, or thinking back to how things were. Joe would so hate that.

I think about all this on the train home.

Eighteen

I fumble for my keys, open the front door. Silence. No one's here. Again.

I dump my bag in my room, fish out my creased and dirty clothes, take them with me back downstairs, and shove them in the washing machine. It strikes me how immaculate the house looks, as if no one actually lives here. No papers on the table, no crumbs anywhere, nothing lying around. Mum's put all my things upstairs in my room. Is it because of the contrast with a student house, or because I've been thinking about the kitchen at Home Farm, that this hits me all over again?

I wish Theo was here with me.

I phone Miranda, but her mobile's on answerphone. I text her instead, and when she doesn't answer I phone her home.

Her grumpy younger brother answers.

'It's Freya. Is Miranda there?'

'No.'

'When will she be back?'

He grunts. 'No idea.'

'Tell her I called.'

'OK.' He puts down the phone.

I feel even more lonely after that. I switch on the computer and fill the house with music. I make toast, and eat it in the sitting room. I read bits of the Sunday newspaper and leave the loose pages all over the floor. I write the postcards for Gramps and Evie, and another for Danny. I never phoned him back, I realise. I think carefully what to say. I tell him about the washed-up whale, and about the lighthouse being for sale. *Love Freya*, I write, and I add three kisses.

My phone bleeps with a text message. But it's from Theo, not Miranda.

You are officially invited to Christmas dinner at Home Farm. Mum says hope you can come.

Yes! I text back immediately. **Thanks xx**

And he texts me back, just as fast:

Take care, bright star.

I stare at the words for ages, tingling with excitement. *Bright star*, like in the poem. I turn up the music, and dance over to the window.

It's dark outside already.

Bit by bit, a familiar Sunday afternoon gloom begins to descend on me. Eventually, I draw all the curtains and turn on the lights. I go up to my room and check my notebook to see what homework I need to do before tomorrow. I open my Biology textbook and start to read the chapter for Monday's class, but it's hard to concentrate for long. I keep seeing Theo's pale face, with his dark eyes, and the long fringe of dark hair. I can still smell his woollen coat, hear the echo of his voice reading poems. I think of how I held him while he cried.

The car draws up outside. I listen to the slam of doors, and footsteps up the path. Mum turns her key in the lock, opens the front door and calls out, 'Freya! You home?'

I put down my book and walk slowly to the top of the stairs. 'Where've you two been?'

'Just lunch out. Did you have a good time, darling?'

'Yes thanks.'

'I expected you to phone us for a lift home,' Mum says.

'No. It was fine.'

Dad comes up behind Mum and puts his arms around her. She leans back against him, giggling softly. She'll have had wine with her lunch. Just one glass makes her like that.

I turn away. She's not listening to me, really. It doesn't matter that I'm not telling the truth.

'They've invited me for Christmas dinner,' I blurt out.

'Oh!' For a second, Mum goes pale. But Dad's still holding her, and she recovers herself. 'How . . . how kind of them to ask you.'

'And I said yes,' I add. I go back into my room quickly. I know I've hurt them, but I can't bear to actually see it on their faces.

I force myself to turn the page of my Biology book. Photosynthesis. I make myself read the words. Plain words, facts, science. I imagine a conversation with Theo. *Intellect and rationality: sometimes they come in handy. You can't be feeling all the time, whatever your poet Keats says.*

Mum brings me a cup of tea, later. She comes right in and sits on my bed. 'Freya? It's fine, about Christmas. I want you to know that. I understand, I really do. We need to do things differently. It's a good thing. I'm glad for you.'

'Really?' I swivel round in my chair at the desk.

She has tears in her eyes.

I sit down next to her on the bed, put my arms round her. 'Oh, Mum.'

She burrows her head into my shoulder and hugs me tight.

'I won't go,' I say. 'Not if you are going to be so sad.'

'No. I want you to. It's just what you need. And it will make Dad and me think about what we really want to do, too. Joe wouldn't want us all to be moping around.' She puts on a smile for me. 'It's fine, darling. Really.'

Miranda phones me at bedtime. She sounds furious. 'Where have you *been* all weekend?'

'I tried to phone you this afternoon,' I say. 'Didn't your brother tell you?'

'Never mind that. You had your phone switched off the whole of Saturday. Don't deny it. And you certainly weren't with Gabes.'

I don't speak.

'So, are you going to tell me? Or what's the point of us being friends? Come to think of it, Freya, there isn't any point. I've had enough.'

And that's it. She's gone.

Nineteen

'There you go. Uno cappuccino!' Gabes says. We settle ourselves down at our usual table in the Boston café, next to the window, at the end of the college day.

The door opens and Miranda comes in with Charlie and the rest of their crowd from Geography; she deliberately goes to sit at a different table.

We're still not speaking. It's been four days: the longest time we've kept up being angry with each other *ever*, since we first became friends. I can tell she's trying to listen in on my conversation with Gabes, though, from the way she's sitting, half turned round in her chair. She's not really paying attention to Charlie.

'I hear you're coming to ours for Christmas,' Gabes says. 'Mum said.'

I feel myself blushing.

'I hear it was Theo's idea,' Gabes says.

'Well. Yes. He asked me, when I saw him in Oxford.'

'When you went to the Art school Open Day?'

I nod. I feel terrible, lying to Gabes.

Miranda glares at me and goes back to her conversation with Charlie. I'm praying she can't hear my actual words.

Gabes notices her too. 'What's up with her? You two fallen out?'

I sigh. 'Sort of.'

He laughs. 'Lovers' tiff.'

'What do you mean?'

'You and Miranda. The amount of time you two spend together! Though not so much, recently, I've noticed. You weren't with her at the weekend.'

'No.' My heart sinks. Is he about to ask where I was? Any minute now and it's all going to come out.

'Is something wrong? You seem kind of nervous,' Gabes says.

I'm terrified that Miranda's going to say something to Gabes right this minute. She's standing up. But no, she's just going to the counter to order drinks. She doesn't say anything when she goes past us. Her bag bumps the back of my chair deliberately.

Gabes pulls a face.

'She's in a mood with me,' I say.

'Obviously! What have you done?'

'Nothing, really. She'll get over it. I hope.' I change the subject quickly. 'So, Christmas. You sure it's OK?'

'Course. The more the merrier: you know Maddie.'

'I don't mean her, I mean for you. It's just that, well, my last few Christmases at home have been totally awful. Me being the only child. No Joe.'

Gabes looks sympathetic. 'I can imagine,' he says.

'And it's usually fun at ours. Lots of people, anyway. You'll have a good time.' He's silent for a while.

I finish my coffee and spoon up the milky froth at the bottom of the cup.

'I'll hear whether I've got my place in London, soon.' Gabes says.

'You're bound to get in.' I make a sad face. 'I've just got to know you, and now you'll be off.'

'Not till next September. And you can visit,' he says. 'Like you visit Theo.'

For a second I'm so taken aback I'm speechless. He knows! How? Did Miranda tell him? Theo?

Gabes gets up. 'Want another coffee? I'm getting me one.'

I shake my head. 'No thanks.' My voice comes out weird. I know my face must be scarlet: I've gone hot all over.

I'm so totally embarrassed I can't think. I watch him standing at the counter ordering his coffee. He turns for a moment, and catches my eye. He's so very good-looking, with his golden, curly hair and startlingly blue eyes, and so very different from Theo you'd never guess they were brothers.

I didn't expect this.

Gabes brings his coffee back to the table and sits down next to me. He stretches his long legs out under the table and sits back in his chair, stirring in a spoonful of sugar, acting too casual, as if he's not bothered.

'I'm sorry,' I say at last. 'I should have told you straight away about meeting up with Theo.'

Gabes frowns. He carries on stirring. 'It's none of my business, really,' he says. 'You're a free agent.'

I wait.

There's a horrible silence before he starts talking again. 'But my *brother*, Freya? A bit insensitive, don't you think? Not even to mention it.'

'It's not like you think.'

'What do I think?'

'Oh, I don't know. This is really embarrassing, Gabes. But you and me, well, we've just been friends all this time, haven't we? I mean, you didn't seem interested in me, not in *that* way . . . least, that's what I thought; not like girl and boyfriend I mean, and of course that's fine, if it's what you want, and it's kind of the same with Theo but . . . except . . .' I run out of words.

'Except?'

'I don't know.' My voice fades.

'He fancied you right from the start, didn't he? I should have realised.' Gabes turns to look me right in the eyes. 'That's so typical of him, you know? He doesn't have a clue what *friendship* means. He's jealous of it, so he has to mess it up for me. It's like a kind of base instinct with him when he can't have something: to destroy it for someone else.'

I look down at the table. I fold the paper napkin over and over, into tight white squares. This is horrible.

'You should be very careful of Theo,' Gabes says slowly, after a long silence.

I don't ask him what he means. He's warning me, and I kind of know he's right, but I don't want to hear any more.

Across the room, Miranda is watching. She half smiles, and turns away.

I feel sick, suddenly. Claustrophobic.

'I need to go,' I say. I grab my coat and my bag and push open the door, out into the street.

I stand for a second on the busy square. The fruit-stall people are packing up. Pigeons are pecking at the scraps in the gutter. The big tree in the middle of the square is twinkling with fairy lights hung along the branches. Above the tall buildings that surround the square, the sky is a deep navy blue.

I blink tears away. This is ridiculous. I haven't done anything wrong. Not really. Have I? I've kept some secrets. Got close to two brothers. It's hardly a crime, is it? Why can't I be friends with both of them?

I glance back at the café. It looks cosy and comforting, all lit up. And then, when I look more carefully, I see Miranda, sitting exactly where I was a few minutes ago, leaning forward, talking to Gabes.

I turn away. I start the walk home alone through the crowded streets. Town's been busy like this since half-term: coachloads of people doing Christmas shopping. I have to push through crowds of tourists staring up at the decorations in the Abbey courtyard. The noise and the people grate on my nerves. I shove and push through the people waiting at the park and ride bus stops, past the queues waiting for the cash machine outside the supermarket, past the church and the library. I start walking home up the hill: the pavements are emptier here, now that I'm passing houses and flats and pubs instead of shops. I begin to calm down.

It's nearly six by the time I get back, but neither Mum or Dad are home. They seem to be working later and later. I remember, as soon I see her note, that Mum said she was going straight from work to a talk at the university to do with her landscape gardening course. There's macaroni cheese ready to be heated up for my supper, and salad in the fridge.

I can't be bothered to heat the food; I eat it straight from the bowl, cold, standing at the kitchen window. I don't eat any salad. I go upstairs and lie on my bed. I don't bother to turn my light on. I stay there for ages. Eventually, I crawl over to the desk, switch on the lamp, haul my bag up on to my lap and look for my homework notebook.

Art coursework due on Monday. Biology test: Friday. That's tomorrow. I pull out my Biology file and start reading the notes. I make myself focus.

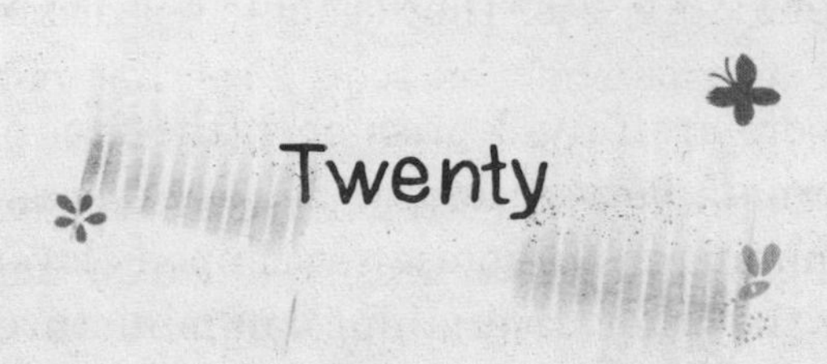

Twenty

'You've got some post,' Mum says as I come in the door after college on Friday. 'Looks like an enormous Christmas card. Wonder who it's from?'

'Mum! You're so nosy!'

I pick up the envelope from the kitchen table and take it upstairs with me. I don't recognise the handwriting.

I open it.

It's from Danny.

Not a card, but an Advent calendar. Not a glitzy one or one with chocolates, but home-made specially for me: he's drawn a picture with pen and ink, painted it, stuck on glitter sprinkles, made the little doors with numbers and everything. The picture is a map of St Ailla, with the beaches and the lighthouse and the post office shop and the farm and campsite and everything. He's drawn tiny Christmas lights along the rigging of the little ferry moored up in the bay.

There's a note on a scrap of paper.

You can open all the doors up to today (whatever

day this gets to you, that is) but then you must promise only to open one a day till Christmas Eve. No cheating! Dan x

The doors are tiny. I prise open the first one with my fingernail, very carefully. Inside, there's a little fish, swimming in turquoise sea. I open eleven doors, one after the other. Everything's in miniature. A tiny border collie dog, like Bess at the farm; a crab pot; a rowing gig; a fire on a beach; three mackerel on a fishing line; my blue notebook; a pebble; my special glass bead; a paper lantern with a candle inside; two wetsuits hanging on a line; a tent. He's drawn each little picture in black ink and then touched in the colours delicately with a watercolour wash. I had no idea he could even draw.

For a split second I'm almost jealous that I didn't have the idea first. But I'd never have thought of making an Advent calendar for Danny. Who now calls himself *Dan*, I notice.

I imagine him poring over the paper, his dark hair falling forwards over his face, concentrating. I stare at the tiny pictures. They bring my island summers so sharply into focus that for a moment I am full of *longing* to be there – to be sitting in Evie and Gramps' solid stone house, or running up to the downs, the sound of the sea drumming in my head. I want to be climbing up, up one of the rocky stacks on the wild side of the island, right to the top, the wind blowing my hair back as I stand, arms outstretched, taking in the whole panorama of our island and all the other islands stretching beyond, dark shapes floating on a bright sea.

Dear Danny. *Dan.*

I am utterly touched – it's the nicest present anyone could have given me, and so totally unexpected. I work out that each of the little pictures is a reference to something we've done together or something I've told him about. I prop the calendar up on my table against the lamp. Just looking at it makes me smile.

But I don't stay happy for long. It's Friday night, and I'm not going anywhere. No one's phoned or texted me. I daren't call Miranda. I have the horrible feeling that she's never going to talk to me again. Right now she's probably out with Charlie and Tabitha and Ellie and everyone – Gabes, even – having fun. I wonder what she's been saying about me. I feel really alone.

Theo will be back at Home Farm this weekend.

But I don't phone him, and he doesn't phone me.

After a while I stop moping and pull myself together. I might as well make the most of my spare evening. I've got loads of work to finish for college. I need to plan what to get for Christmas presents for everyone.

I go looking for Mum. I find her sitting at the desk in her newly painted study with the blue curtains and white walls, a big pad of paper spread out in front of her.

'What can I send Evie and Gramps for Christmas?'

'Something you've made?' Mum says. 'They don't really *need* anything.' She puts her arm round my waist and pulls me closer to her. 'Most of all they'd like to see you, Freya. Perhaps you could arrange a date to go over? The Easter holidays, or spring half-term, when the weather will be better.'

'What are you doing in here?' I ask her.

'Planning out a garden, for a new client. Dad's client, in fact, but they're going to be guinea pigs for my first proper design.'

'Nice.'

'Yes. I'm pleased.' She takes her arm away, and flips back a page to show me what she's done so far. 'I need to get on, Freya. I've got so much to do at the moment.' She looks up at me briefly. 'You're OK, aren't you? I don't seem to have spent much time with you lately. But I guess you've got plenty on too. You're busy with your own friends.'

'I'm fine,' I say, though I'm not. I drift towards the door. I almost tell her about Theo. About Bridie and Gabes and Miranda and *everything*. I'd like to, really. But she's busy working again, head bent low, concentrating on her design. This isn't the right time. I pad downstairs into the kitchen and make myself tea.

I flick through the stack of drawings and paintings in my portfolio. It will need to be something small enough to frame and post. I pull out the one I did back in September, of a girl swimming out to sea, viewed from high up, as if we are looking with a seagull's eye, with the space of air and light between. It's still my favourite.

I rummage through my bits of paper and card to find some mounting board, and get my special knife from my pencil case, for cutting the edges. It's one of the cool things we've learned this term, how to mount a picture properly, with a bevelled edge. It takes two goes to get it right. I turn the board over and in pencil with my best handwriting, I write the title of the painting: *Into the Wild Blue.* I sign my name. It's going to be too heavy to post if I get a wooden frame for it, so I decide not to. I wrap it up in layers of white tissue paper and bubble wrap and then some shiny blue paper from the box of recycled wrapping paper we keep under the stairs. I write on a small square of card: *Happy Christmas to dearest Evie and Gramps with all my love from Freya xxxxx,* wrap the whole thing in brown paper and address the package.

I'll post it tomorrow.

I sort out Mum and Dad's present, next, and then I try to think of something I could send to Danny. I scan in the drawing I did of him in the summer, fishing for mackerel off the rocks. I make it into a card. I don't write much, just *Happy Christmas*, and *love Freya.*

And then I think about Miranda: even if she isn't speaking to me, I still have to send her something. I can't bear not to. So I make another card for her from the same little sketch of Beady Pool that I used as the inspiration for Mum and Dad's watercolour painting. Next I go through a load of photos to find one of us together, that I can print out and frame for her as a present. If we ever see each other again, that is.

Dad comes back from his latest work trip at about ten thirty; I hear voices, him laughing with Mum downstairs, the chink of wine glasses, and then music drifts upstairs and I can't hear anything else. I check my phone for the millionth time but there are still no messages.

Is Miranda waiting for me to say sorry? I text the words, and wait, but nothing comes back from her. Just before I go to sleep, I send a message to Danny.

Thank you for the beautiful calendar xxx

In the morning when I go downstairs, I find Mum and Dad already up, drinking coffee at the kitchen table.

Dad smiles at me over the Saturday review pages. 'Hello, stranger! OK?'

'Fine.'

'Got plans for the day, Freya?' Mum asks.

'Thought I'd go swimming,' I say. 'I haven't been for ages.'

'Great idea. Want a lift down? I'll be going shopping later.'

I shake my head. 'I'll go early, before the pool's too busy. I can go on my bike.'

'Town will be mad this morning,' Dad says. 'Take care on the roads.'

I've forgotten about gloves, so by the time I've got halfway to the canal path my hands are frozen. This way along the towpath is a short cut and avoids the worst traffic on the London Road. It's pretty, all covered in frost, the sun breaking through the mist. I ring my bell to warn the dog walkers as I bowl past. I duck under the first two bridges. At the third one I stop: this is the turning for the track down to the riverside path to the leisure centre. If I went straight on, I'd pass by our old house, with its steep garden going down in terraces to the canal . . . the house where we were so happy together, with Joe . . .

I turn off down the track. The river is high. The water swirls and eddies, dangerous and mud-brown, bearing whole trees along in the swift current. You'd never imagine you could swim in it in the summer, or that anyone might even want to.

It's been a while since I've swum in an indoor pool. The sounds echo round your head, the water seems dead and sludgy. It stinks of chlorine. But after a while I get into a rhythm up and down the pool in one of the roped-off lanes, and it's good to be making my body really work. After about thirty lengths of front crawl, my mind begins to calm down. My thoughts stop racing. It's as if the jagged edges have been ironed out. I breathe more deeply. Let it all go, I tell myself. Miranda, Gabes, all that. None of it matters. Things will be all right. I do another ten lengths, breaststroke this time. I float for a while on my back.

The clock ticks round. The pool begins to fill up with screaming kids, families. I climb out. My legs feel wobbly and achey from the exercise: I suppose I've got out of the habit the last few weeks. It doesn't take long to lose fitness. Under the shower I start to remember all the things I don't like about the changing rooms: the dirty floor; the hairs clogging the drains. Queuing to use the hairdryers. I put my wet towel and swimsuit and goggles into my bag and go outside. It's only eleven fifteen.

I wheel my bike along the road into the town centre. It's heaving with Christmas shoppers. I stop off at the post office to send my parcel to St Ailla: there's a huge queue, and they've got some stupid new system. I take the ticket for my turn and sit down on one of the new seats, the parcel on my lap. Staring at the address makes me think about Evie and Gramps having a quiet island Christmas, without Joe or me, and my eyes suddenly fill with tears.

My phone bleeps with a new message.

Theo!

Film at 7.30ish? Meet inside cinema?

Yes! I text back.

He must have come back from Oxford last night with Beth. And he's thinking about me.

The day begins to get brighter.

It takes me ages to decide what to wear. I'm not normally so self-conscious. I try a short skirt with black leggings and boots, and then change back to jeans. Nothing looks right. I brush my hair a million times, to make it shiny, and try pinning it up loosely with my silver butterfly clip, and then I give up on that too.

Mum looks up as I slip past her door. 'You going out, Freya? I haven't even thought about supper yet!'

'It's OK,' I say. 'I had a sandwich earlier.'

'Where are you going?'

'Just a film.'

'Don't walk back by yourself if it's late. Call us for a lift if you need one.'

Dad's outside in the garage, making something. He waves as I go past. 'Have fun!'

A kind of bleakness washes over me again, like last

night. It's as if I don't properly belong here, in this house. It isn't a family house. Ours isn't a real family any more. I feel as if I might just blow away: there's nothing holding me down, keeping me safe.

I arrive at the cinema five minutes early. For the next twenty-five minutes I imagine he's not going to turn up after all, and that everyone going past will know I'm a total loser with no friends. For a second I think I glimpse Miranda in a crowd of people going into Screen One. I look away quickly and pretend to study the posters on the wall.

At last I see him: pale face, dark clothes, messy hair. He weaves through the crowds of people in the foyer towards me.

'You're really late!' I say.

'Am I? Sorry. Got caught up with stuff. Shall we get tickets, then?'

The two decent films are sold out, and there's no way I want to sit through either of the others: a meant-to-be-funny one about a teacher and a nativity play, or a dreary action movie.

Theo looks cross.

'It's your fault for being so late,' I tell him.

'Well, since you were waiting here, why didn't you just get two tickets?'

'Because we hadn't agreed which film! Honestly, Theo!'

'You should have chosen one you wanted to see, seeing as you are so picky.'

Already we're pitching into an argument. We seem

to do that every time we first meet. I bite back my reply. No point making things worse.

'What now? I've got the van. We can go somewhere else,' Theo says.

'The van?'

'Mum's van. Beth wouldn't let me take her car.'

'I didn't know you could drive!'

'I don't need to in Oxford. But I can.'

For some reason I feel slightly scared. It's not that I don't trust him, exactly . . . If Maddie lends him her van she must reckon he's safe. But he's still got that angry look in his eyes, a bit reckless and wild, which makes me wary.

'You're too young to go to a pub for a drink. You don't want to see a film. What *do* you want?' Theo says.

'I want you to stop being so mean! None of that is my fault. Why don't we just walk round town and find a café that's open? We could get something to eat.'

'Fine.' He turns his collar up as we go out into the cold, pulls his scarf round more tightly. He links arms with me. Gradually, he relaxes a bit.

But I'm still so tense. It's all going wrong. I feel stupid and too young. Not clever or *entertaining* enough.

We walk up through the centre of town towards the park. The huge trees at one end are lit up with the glow from the lights in a big marquee.

'Hey, the outdoor ice rink's back!' I say. 'Like last year. We could go skating!'

Theo shrugs.

'Please? Be a *bit* enthusiastic.'

We queue up to pay for the next slot. There's a bar; Theo gets a bottle of cider while we wait for our turn.

Music blares out from the speakers in the middle, and the machines that pump cold air over the fake ice hum loudly too, so we have to shout to talk at all. In the end we give up and we simply skate together, arm in arm, like I did with Miranda that time. I show him the steps I know, and how to go backwards, and then we just join in with all the other people going round and round, skates finding the grooves made by everyone else, all flowing in the same direction, a current of people joined together by movement. It's like swimming, almost, graceful and effortless.

'That was surprisingly fun!' Theo says as we step off the ice at the end of our turn. His cheeks are flushed, his eyes bright.

I'm giddy with it all: the movement, the lights and music, the crowds, the rush of happiness as he gives me a hug.

We walk back through the park the long way, under the avenue of cherry trees and across the frosty grass in darkness. Away from the marquee, the park is almost silent. We hold hands. We run, and slide on the grass and laugh when Theo skids right over, and pulls me with him. My boots are covered in mud by the time we get to the path. We walk down through the town, back to where Theo's parked the van.

'I'll take you home,' Theo says.

'It's OK,' I say. 'It's not far to walk.'

'But not on your own, not in the dark this late.'

'It's not that late!'

'What's the matter? Don't you want me to see where you live? Or is it because of your parents? They won't approve?'

I laugh, embarrassed. I'm not about to explain that they don't know anything about him yet; that I've never mentioned him once. And of course they wouldn't approve of him! Or of me, going out with someone who's twenty-one. Who smokes and drinks. Who has a scary fascination with a dead girl.

We scrape the ice off the van windscreen. Theo unlocks the door for me to get in. Sitting high up on the front seat reminds me of the time Maddie picked up me and Gabes after the bike accident, but I don't tell Theo that, either.

He starts up the engine. It takes lots of revs to get going. 'It's got cold,' Theo says. He pulls out of the space. 'Now, which direction?'

He drives quite slowly and carefully, not at all like I expected. He stops at the top of my road for me to get out. 'There. Now no one need know who you've been with all evening.'

'Theo! Don't say that!' I kiss him goodbye. His mouth is soft, delicious. He tastes of apples.

'I'll be busy for the next few days,' Theo says. 'But I'll see you on Christmas Day. No need to bring presents or anything. Family rule, for house guests. Mum said to tell you that.'

'Don't you have presents?'

'Only from Mum and Dad. There's too many of us.'

'Who else will be there?'

'All of us – Mum, Dad, Laura and Tom; Beth and the babies and Will; Gabes, Kit, me, you, Kit's friend Liu because she can't go home to her parents this year; two aunties and uncles and my cousins . . . I think that's everyone, though knowing Mum she'll pick up a few extras between now and Christmas Day.'

I watch the van as Theo drives away. He just takes it for granted that he has this big busy family, loads of friends. He doesn't know how lucky he is.

Back home, I wonder briefly whether Bridie ever spent Christmas at Home Farm, and whether Theo will be thinking about her this Christmas. I remember what Gabes said about Maddie collecting *waifs and strays*.

Later, lying in bed, I have a horrible thought. Am I one of them? Does she think of me like that, too? Do they all?

Twenty-one

College finishes at midday on the Friday before Christmas. At break, I finally pluck up courage and text Gabes. I've thought about it loads; made my decision last night in bed.

Can we meet somewhere? I'd really like to talk. Please? Freya.

He texts back straight away. **Coffee at the Jazz café at 1? Gx**

The kiss gives me hope. Not for a real kiss, I don't mean. Just that things can be OK between us. For some silly reason I've got dressed up specially: dress, leggings, boots. Maybe because it makes me feel more confident or something. But I get there too early, so I still end up nervous, waiting for him to show.

Everyone else will be at the Boston, celebrating the end of term. I'm glad Gabes chose this place instead. It's warm and steamy, smells of bacon breakfasts. It reminds me a bit of the café in Exeter, where I first saw Gabes and his family, before I knew anything about them, except that it's not as busy. There are loads of free tables. I sit down at one near the big plate-glass window and order a coffee.

I watch him cross the road and walk into the café, bang on one o'clock.

He smiles as he comes over. 'Cappuccino?'

'I've already ordered,' I say. 'But thanks.'

He sits down opposite me, chucks his bag on to the wooden floor. 'Well?'

I blurt it all out in a rush. 'I couldn't just turn up at Home Farm without talking to you first. I'm sorry I rushed off last time. I feel really bad about everything. Not being straight with you about seeing Theo. All that. I didn't mean to hurt you. I mean, if you were hurt. Perhaps you weren't. But anyway.'

He reaches out and touches my hand. 'It's OK, Freya,' he says. 'Calm down.'

I go hot. Why do I find it so difficult to talk about these things?

He's still smiling. I notice all over again how good-looking he is, how clear and direct and sunny.

I have another go. 'And the thing is, well, I'm not trying to make an excuse or anything, but we've only ever been friends, haven't we?'

He frowns slightly. 'Only? Isn't friendship important, Freya?'

I go hot again. 'Yes! Of course it is. What I mean is, well, we weren't going out together or anything, were we? Like, girlfriend and boyfriend.' The words sound ridiculous now I say them. 'I never really knew what you thought of me.'

Gabes looks surprised. 'Isn't it obvious I like you?

Why would I hang out with you, otherwise? And I don't know why it didn't become *more* than friends. I guess that extra spark just didn't happen, did it? You can't force it. And that was fine by me.'

It's hard, hearing him say that about the *extra spark*. But we didn't give it a chance, did we? *I* didn't, I suppose I mean. First his broken foot, and then Theo turning up . . .

Gabes is still talking. 'What I didn't like was the way Theo behaved. Moving in on you like he did. Like, wanting you almost *because* you were my friend. And knowing what I do about him, I was worried for you, too. Especially when you started being so secretive.'

It's hard to keep looking at him.

Gabes pushes his chair back a bit. 'So, it was Theo I was angry with, really; not you. But that's all over with. There's no point hanging on to that stuff. He's my brother. I should know him well enough by now!'

'He's very different from you,' I say. 'You're not like brothers at all.'

Gabes doesn't say anything for a while. We sip our coffees. I stare out of the window. It's beginning to rain.

'I'm sorry I wasn't more open and honest,' I say. 'I still feel bad about that.'

Gabes shrugs. 'It's OK. Really. Anyway, you and I will stay friends longer than Theo and you do.'

That shocks me. 'Why do you say that?'

'He gets obsessed with things, ideas, people. Then it burns out. He finds someone – something – else. That's how he is.'

I think about that. Oddly, it doesn't really upset me. Deep down, I know what Gabes has said is probably true.

'He seems so troubled,' I say. 'He's still very upset about Bridie. I thought I might be able to help him. Because of what I went through, when Joe died.'

Gabes sighs. 'Well, you can try. He needs to help himself, really. But maybe you can make a difference. It's nice, I guess, that you want to.'

We're both quiet. We finish our coffees.

I start talking again. The thoughts have been whirling round my head for so long that it's a relief to get them out. 'I had this idea, that perhaps if I went with Theo to a special place that had meant something to Bridie, I could help him say goodbye to her,' I say. 'To help him heal.'

He looks doubtful. 'Maybe,' he says. 'But you should be careful how much time you spend with him. Think about what you need, too. Don't get dragged under by Theo's problems. You have to do what's right for you, first.'

He glances at his watch.

'Do you need to go?' I ask.

'In a minute. I'm glad we met up and talked. And it will be good, you coming for Christmas Day.'

'Are you sure? Even with Theo there too?'

'Sure. We're still friends, remember?' He stands up, picks up his bag. I get up too. He puts his arms round me and hugs me. 'Don't worry about things so much, Freya!'

I hug him back. For some reason, him being so kind makes me want to cry.

'See you Christmas Day, then!' He hugs me one more time.

He picks up his bag and leaves. I watch him go. I don't feel like I expected to at all. I'm more sad than relieved. Still, Gabes is right. It's good that we met up. I did well to make it happen.

I've got to be more like Gabes. Put things behind me. Stop dwelling on everything. Look forward, instead.

Twenty-two

Dad slows down and stops the car at the top of the drive. 'I'll just come in and wish them all Happy Christmas,' he says. 'I won't hang around long, don't worry.'

'No, Dad. Please? They'll be really busy. There are loads of people coming.' I lean over and kiss his cheek. 'Thanks for the lift. Have a lovely time with Mum.' I open the car door before he can say anything else, climb out and wave, but don't look back.

The air smells of wood smoke. It's frosty again today, and the ground is still frozen solid at midday. A pale sun shines weakly through the copse of trees above the house. I walk slowly down the slippery drive into the courtyard, take a deep breath, and walk round to the real front door, rather than the usual back way into the kitchen. I ring the old bell; wait, heart beating fast. I'm excited and nervous at the same time. Someone's tied a big bunch of larch and holly and ivy to the door knocker with a strip of gold ribbon: I imagine Maddie picking the green sprigs from her wild garden. I know everything will be like this: home-made, and perfect.

The door opens. 'Freya! Welcome! Happy Christmas.' Nick steps forward to hug me. He feels warm and solid, more substantial than my own father. 'Freya's here!' he calls.

Theo's hovering at the bottom of the stairs behind his dad, but it's Gabes who steps forward and hugs me. 'Hi, come on in.' Gabes hangs my coat up for me. The three of us go into the sitting room. I glance at Theo. He seems OK.

'Oh wow! It looks amazing!'

It's exactly how I imagined it. On every shelf there are vases and jugs filled with branches of yew and holly and fronds of some other evergreen tree with tiny sweet-smelling white flowers. Christmas cards hang on strips of red ribbon along the walls; white lights drape artistically along the mantelpiece above the big fireplace in the sitting room; candles in star-shaped holders glint and flicker from the dark corners. Next to the window a real Christmas tree as tall as the ceiling shines with gold fairy lights and glass baubles. The dark green branches are hung with wooden angels and soft fabric birds and all kinds of weird and wonderful decorations.

'See this?' I made it at primary school!' Theo points to a miniature stained-glass window dangling on a low branch. 'And Gabes painted these when he was about seven.' He touches a string of funny technicoloured kings on camels and laughs. 'You can see what a brilliant *artist* he was already.'

'Freya!' Maddie comes hurrying downstairs and into the sitting room. She's wearing a dark red velvet dress, her hair tied up with gold ribbon. She smiles at me. 'Lovely to see you. Happy Christmas, darling!' She hugs me tight. 'You look gorgeous. Did your dad bring you? Is he still here?'

'He dropped me at the top of the drive,' I say quickly. 'He and Mum are going out for the afternoon.' I don't want to think about them now, just the two of them doing their own thing: a long country walk and a candlelit supper together.

'Oh well,' Maddie says. 'We're very grateful to your parents, lending you to us for the day!'

Theo makes a face behind her and Gabes laughs. Apart from that, they seem to be on their best behaviour. They are both delightful: funny, attentive.

'Time to lay the table,' Theo says, and I follow him into the kitchen.

Beth's face is red from checking the roast potatoes in the hot oven. 'Welcome, Freya! Happy Christmas!'

'It smells fantastic!' I say. 'Shall I do something?'

'No need,' Beth says. 'All under control, more or less. Theo, get Freya something to drink. Have you met the cousins yet?'

I shake my head.

'Gabes, why don't you take Freya and introduce her to everyone before we sit down for dinner?'

Theo grins at me as I follow Gabes back out of the kitchen. I smile back. I start to relax about the three of us: Gabes, Theo and me.

I meet his aunties, Kate and Hannah, and their

husbands, Tim and Simon, and the cousins – eleven-year-old Ellie, and Charlie, who is just a bit older than Beth's twins.

We find Kit upstairs in his room, listening to music with his friend Liu, a girl from his school with beautiful straight black hair and brown eyes. She shakes hands with me as if I am a grown-up.

Gabes stops halfway along the landing, when we're alone again. 'Theo's already had too much to drink,' he says.

'He seemed fine downstairs just now.'

'Just don't take him too seriously, OK? If he starts talking too much. He sometimes says stuff.'

'What sort of stuff?'

'You know; he gets gloomy. But don't let it get to you. Better to stay with everyone, you know, together? To help jolly him along.'

I shrug. 'OK.'

Later, I watch Theo as he arranges the crackers and napkins and lays out the cutlery. He looks perfectly fine and normal. A bit flushed, perhaps. When I look more closely, I see his eyes are extra bright, sort of glittery. Maybe Gabes is right after all. But then it's time for everyone to gather for the big dinner, and I stop thinking about it.

We've got place names to show us where to sit. Beth has put me between Phoebe, in her high chair, and Gabes, so I can help Phoebe with her food. It's nice to feel useful. Theo is opposite. There are so many of us that it's impossible to have one big conversation. We pull the crackers, put on the paper crowns and read out the jokes, everyone taking turns.

Nick stands up. 'Here's to health and happiness, to family and friendship!'

We clink glasses for the toast. It goes quiet for a minute when we all begin eating, and then the talking starts up again. Tom, Laura's boyfriend, tops up the glasses with champagne. I take a tiny sip.

I'm so happy: being surrounded by people, by a proper family, who don't even once make me feel left out or as if I don't really belong. I notice the way Maddie and Nick make such efforts to talk to Liu, even though she's so shy and quiet. Laura helps Beth feed Erin, and Kit entertains little Charlie when he's had enough of sitting still. Gabes makes a whole family of paper frogs for the little ones. It's noisy and messy and fun, even when Theo starts arguing with Nick and Tom.

'Stop it, all of you!' Maddie says. 'Not at the table, not at Christmas.' She turns back to say something to Liu.

It's dark outside, now. We've done the clearing up, and had coffee, played silly family games (charades; *Articulate*, in teams; a slightly drunken version of hunt the thimble, with a champagne cork instead of a thimble).

'We play the same games each year.' Theo rolls his eyes.

'I don't mind. I think it's lovely, having family traditions.'

'Who's up for Murder in the Dark, next?' Kit says.

Maddie groans. 'No way am I crawling around in the dark at this stage of the evening!'

Nick laughs. 'Why don't all you kids play, while we watch a film?'

Kit and Gabes hunt for paper and pens and then make a big performance of drawing the letters on scraps of paper that are all exactly the same size, so no one can guess who the Murderer is. Kit tries to explain the rules to Liu, but she still doesn't understand.

I've played this game before, but not for a while. My heart starts thumping as soon as I start unfolding my bit of paper. It's like being little again. But I haven't picked one of the special ones: there's just an O written in Kit's spidery writing in the middle.

We troop upstairs on the landing to the carpeted area between the two halves of the old house, where there are two sofas and a chair. Theo turns off the lights.

Gabes runs back to turn off the downstairs ones too.

'It's too dark now! I can't see anything!' Liu says.

'That's the point!'

'I'm scared!' Ellie whispers.

And so am I, even though it is too ridiculous to say aloud. It is so completely dark that I cannot tell who is who. I'm waiting for the heavy-handed cross shape on my back, but even an arm brushing against mine feels frightening. Gabes mutters something, and Beth shushes him. The room is full of dark shadowy movement as we circle round, waiting for the Murderer to strike.

We move round the room, giggling, trying to avoid bumping into each other. Beth – at least, I think it's her – sits on one of the chairs and stays there.

Someone's breathing heavily, right by my ear. My body tenses. Prickles run down my spine. A hand strokes my cheek, and for a moment I can't tell who it is. I turn towards the dark shadow: Theo's mouth brushes mine. 'Not now,' I whisper. 'Not here!'

He moves away again.

The suspense is horrible. It lasts too long, and then at last there's a melodramatic, blood-curdling cry: Theo crashes to the floor.

Kit turns on the lights. 'No one move!' He begins his questions, in best detective style.

We play five times, and three out of those, Theo is the victim, murdered by first Gabes, then Kit, and finally by Beth. Is it random, a coincidence? Or are they all using the game, somehow, to express some deep-running emotion? Theo seems to think so. 'You don't have to hit so hard,' he complains. Liu and Kit are the other two victims. I'm slightly miffed that no one chooses me.

'Now what?' Kit asks.

'I'm going to get a drink,' Beth says.

'Let's play Man Hunt.'

'What's that?'

'Outside, with torches. We make two teams, and the aim is to be the first team back to base. You catch the others out by shining the torch on them.'

'We'll need coats. It's freezing!'

Neither Liu nor Ellie want to play, so it's Kit,

Laura and Tom, Theo, Gabes and me left. Two teams of three.

'You pick first, Freya,' Laura says.

'Kit.'

Kit chooses Gabes. So that's our team.

Theo pulls the back door shut behind us.

Stepping into the courtyard it's like entering a whole different world. It's not as dark as I expected because the sky is clear, sprinkled with stars. A three-quarters moon shines silver over the trees and fields, the cobbles and stone walls. Frost glitters on the wind-screen of the van parked up next to the barn. It's icy; totally still. For a second we are all dumbstruck, magicked by the frozen silence.

Laura kisses Tom: the sound seems magnified in the cold night and Gabes and Kit both laugh out loud.

'Shut up, morons,' Tom says.

'Tom!'

'Well, honestly.'

'Come on, then, let's decide where base is,' Kit says.

'The orchard, in the summerhouse.'

'Everyone got a torch?'

'Five minutes for everyone to spread out,' Kit says. 'Game starts when I shout.'

Gabes tugs my hand. 'Come on, Freya!'

I follow him across the yard, up the drive and towards the copse. In the moonlight, we are clearly visible, but up under the trees the darkness absorbs us into itself. My breath makes smoke clouds. Already, my fingers are icy.

An owl calls. Or a person pretending to be an owl. Shadows criss-cross the drive, the yard. My heart pumps warm blood round my body. I strain forward, all senses alert, listening.

'Go!' Kit yells.

Gabes has crept closer to me. He holds me back by the arm. 'Wait. Don't rush.'

Torchlight flickers out across the field: 'Got you!' someone shouts.

'Now!'

I step out quietly out from my hiding place under the trees. Someone moves across the yard next to the barn, and for a second I think of turning on my torch beam to catch them, but all my instincts are to stay safe, hidden by the dark. Gabes is still somewhere behind me: I can hear his feet rustling through dead leaves. I creep forward again.

Something steps out of the shadows, a hand covers my mouth before I can scream as my arm twists painfully back. Theo's hot breath comes on my face: the sharp stink of alcohol. 'What were you doing up there? With Gabes?' he hisses.

'Nothing. It's a game, Theo. Now let go of my arm. That hurts.'

He loosens his grip.

I pull my arm into my chest, rub the sore place. I can sense Theo's agitation. It makes me afraid. I look back, but there's no sign of Gabes now. Further down the drive, a light flashes, someone shouts out: Laura's been caught.

'Come on,' I say to Theo. 'Shine the torch, seeing as you've caught me. That's the game, isn't it?'

'Why didn't you choose me first, for your team?' Theo pulls me up close again.

I shiver in the dark. 'Theo, this is silly. We're just playing. It's supposed to be fun.'

He's so close I can feel the pulse of his heart against my hand. He puts one hand on my hair, winds it round, so it prickles and pulls against my scalp.

'Ouch! Stop hurting me, Theo!'

'I have caught you now.' His voice sounds strange.

'Let go or I will yell out.'

He lets my hair trickle through his fingers. I run away from him, slipping on the frosty drive.

'Caught!' Tom shouts, shining his torch on my face. 'Only Gabes to get, and we'll have won.'

I join Laura and Kit in the summerhouse. We huddle together for warmth. Laura has found an old blanket and wraps it round us. We listen as Tom's footsteps get quieter, moving up towards the trees. Kit is furious that he was first to be caught, impatient for the game to finish so we can begin all over again.

'It's a strange sort of game,' I say.

'We played it night after night, when Gabes was about fourteen,' Kit says. 'I was only about eleven and I was terrified but also so happy and excited that they'd let me join in for once. We were all deadly serious. Waiting in the dark, it felt real. Not like a game at all.'

Torchlight flickers through the trees, a zigzag of light. Lights tumble over each other. Tom yells out, 'Gabes! You're caught! Come back!'

They walk slowly back down to join us. Theo's with them.

‘We should change the teams,’ Theo says. ‘I’ll go with Freya and Laura this time.’

There’s such a strange note in his voice that no one dares challenge him. That’s how he gets his own way. They’re all a bit scared of him. I run my hand over the back of my neck, where Theo hurt it.

‘It’s much too cold to play out any longer,’ Laura says. ‘I’m going in. Tom?’

He follows her. The rest of us watch the bright square of light spread out over the cobbles as the kitchen door opens, and then fold back into darkness, as it slams shut.

‘Kit and Gabes versus Freya and me,’ Theo says. ‘Ten minutes to disperse, winners are first team back to base without being caught.’ He takes my hand. ‘Ready?’

We run up the drive, feet slipping, and at the top of the hill where the drive meets the lane Theo stops for a second and pulls me in for a kiss. He seems fierce, almost: that glittery quality I’ve seen in him before. Slightly scary. But it’s exciting, too, and I don’t want him to stop. He slips his hands in the space between the buttons on my coat, and then up under my top. I shiver: his hands are freezing next to my bare skin.

‘Let’s run away!’ Theo says. ‘Let’s never go back! Come away with me, Freya!’

I know he’s joking, don’t I? It seems stupid, feeble, to remonstrate, to say it’s too cold, too silly: where would we go, and why? I pull back slightly.

‘Where’s your sense of adventure, Freya?’ That edge is back in his voice.

'I'm numb with cold. And we're supposed to be playing a game. It must be ten minutes by now.'

In the moonlight I can see his face, disappointed.

'Come on. Let's catch the others, Theo.'

'Bridie would have said yes,' Theo says, very quietly. 'She'd have suggested it first.'

'But I'm not Bridie,' I snap. 'And Bridie's dead.' I start running, slipping and sliding on the ice, tears beginning to spill. Once I'm in the yard, I turn the torch on.

Kit and Gabes are both huddled under the blanket in the summerhouse. Kit looks at me in the thin beam of the torchlight. 'What happened? Where were you? You just disappeared. We won, anyway.'

'I'm freezing,' I say. 'I need to go inside.'

'We'll come with you,' Gabes says. 'Where's Theo?'

'Up on the lane, still.'

'Typical. Shall I go and tell him the game's over?' Kit says.

'Leave him to stew,' Gabes says. 'He can look after himself.'

It's late. Theo still hasn't come back. No one else seems worried; the adults don't seem to have noticed, and I can't be the one to tell them. Gabes says to stop worrying, that Theo often goes off, it doesn't mean anything. But I can't help my stomach churning with anxiety about him, about what he might do. It brings back what happened with my brother, when he disappeared that night . . . and even though Theo is nothing like Joe, and we are nowhere near the sea, or boats, and nothing is the same . . . despite knowing all of this, a horrible sense of dread seeps into my bones.

I join the few people still in the sitting room. Nick and Maddie and the aunts and uncles have gone to bed already.

Beth pats the sofa next to her. 'Your cheeks are bright pink from the cold, Freya! And your eyes look all sparkly!'

Laura puts another log on the fire. 'We've all got drinks. Do you want one? Or Gabes will make you something hot, won't you, Gabes? Hot chocolate?'

'Yes please,' I say.

'And for me,' Kit says.

I turn to look at Beth. 'Theo is still outside,' I start to say.

She humphs. 'He's probably gone for a midnight commune with nature, or a swim or something equally mad.'

'He wouldn't. Swim? When it's this cold?'

Beth laughs. 'Who knows? He'll be fine.'

'Shouldn't we go and look for him? It's so dangerous, in cold water, by yourself.'

'I don't think he'd really be so stupid, not even Theo.' She looks at me. She's speaking very quietly, so no one else can hear. 'He'll be trying to impress you, one way or another. How brave he is, or something. You know he's . . . he's a bit obsessed with you? I was confused at first, because I thought you and Gabes were together . . . But when I gave him a lift home from Oxford, Theo talked about you the whole way, practically.'

I don't know what to say to that. I could tell her it's Bridie he's obsessed with, really. Not me. But I don't.

'I've watched you both, today,' Beth says softly. 'You like him too, don't you?'

Before I can answer, the door swings open and Gabes comes in carrying a tray of steaming mugs of hot chocolate. I take mine, sip it slowly. My hands and toes begin to thaw. I'm relieved that Gabes came in and interrupted Beth and me. What could I have possibly said to her about Theo? I do like him, yes, but he scares me, too . . .

Kit pulls the box for Pictionary from under the coffee table and starts sorting out pencils and paper. 'Everyone going to play?'

'Freya and me can be a team,' Beth says. 'You and Gabes, and Tom and Laura, yes?'

Kit throws the dice and the game begins.

I give a huge yawn. I'm warm and cosy now, and very sleepy.

'You look ready for bed!' Beth laughs. 'Do you want to go on up?'

'Which room am I sleeping in?'

'You can choose; there's a spare mattress in our room, if you don't mind being woken up really early by the babies. Or there's the space between the two halves of the house, where we played murder in the dark. Near Theo's room.'

'Did Theo come in?'

'I don't know. Shall we see?'

I pad upstairs behind Beth.

She checks the babies as we go past, and then goes on down the passage way to Theo's door. She knocks, waits, opens it. Empty. 'Why don't we bring the mattress along here, in the space on the landing? Then you'll hear him when he comes back. I'm sure he will. It's much too cold to sleep outside tonight.'

'What if he doesn't? If he's hurt or something?'

Beth yawns. 'I haven't got the energy to go traipsing off in the dark looking for him now. And he'd be furious. He'll be back in his own time, Freya. Really.'

We tiptoe into the babies' room so I can get the mattress and sleeping bag. Both of them are sleeping soundly on their backs, their little hands up by their heads, totally relaxed and open. Beth leans over the cots and strokes their soft heads gently. We carry the mattress between us and put it down on the carpet in the corner under the eaves.

'Now get some sleep. See you in the morning. Breakfast will be help-yourself, any time you want.' Beth kisses me; she strokes my hair too, as if I'm one of her children. 'Night night.'

The heating has gone off hours before; the house is cold. I clean my teeth quickly in the bathroom, hurry back and slither down into the sleeping bag. I'm meaning to stay awake, till I hear Theo's safely back, but I can't . . . my eyes are heavy, I'm drifting. I have that odd sensation of dropping . . . falling . . .

Twenty-three

I wake in the darkness with a lurch. My heart thuds with heavy fear. I lie awake in the dark, straining to hear sounds – any small clue that Theo's home. His door is ajar, like it was before. Is there a light on downstairs? Perhaps the noise of the kitchen door woke me?

But the house is silent, all except for the creaking and rustling of an ancient house where the wooden floorboards, the solid beams and rafters sigh and settle as the temperature drops.

How long is it till morning?

The sense that I'm not in my house, with my own family, steals over me, bit by bit. I long, suddenly and totally, to be somewhere more familiar and safe. The place I'm longing for at this moment isn't the new house with Mum and Dad, but the solid stone house on St Ailla with Evie and Gramps. In my mind's eye I can see it vividly: the slate-tiled roof and the thick walls, the wooden gate and the path through the front garden to the door. I imagine the wind blowing a gale, the booming sound of the sea crashing on the rocks. It is never silent.

And if I was there now, I'd be getting up and going downstairs; Evie would hear me, and she'd come down too, and I'd tell her . . .

Tell her everything.

About Theo, and Bridie. About Gabes, and Beth . . . this family that isn't my family, however much I wish it was.

There! It must have been the sound of the back door, after all, that first woke me. The stairs creak as someone treads heavily up them, and along the landing. I wait, holding my breath, but eyes tight shut, pretending to be asleep.

Theo brushes against my mattress as he squeezes past and goes into his room. I listen to him undressing, pulling the duvet up around him, moving his pillow to get comfy. The bed squeaks every time he shifts or turns over.

It goes quiet.

I open my eyes.

Theo's standing at the bedroom doorway, watching me. His eyes glint in the dark. It's seriously spooky.

'You *are* awake. I knew you were!' he says.

'I was worried about you,' I whisper. 'When you didn't come back.'

'That makes a change,' Theo says. 'I don't suppose anyone else was.'

'Where have you been all this time?'

'I went to see if the stream was frozen. It wasn't, or

only a tiny bit at the edges, not thick enough to take my weight.'

I suck in my breath, imagining him walking on ice, slipping through . . . People die, doing that.

'Then I just walked for hours. Ended up at the railway.'

He's deliberately frightening me.

'Why?' I whisper.

'She told me to.'

'Who did?'

'Bridie, of course.'

I don't speak. I remember what he said before, about hearing voices. Her voice, telling him to do things.

He laughs, a hollow laugh. 'But there were no trains. Because it's Christmas Day.'

'Theo,' I say. 'Stop this.'

'Stop what, sweet Freya?'

'This crazy talk. You don't mean it. You're winding me up. Very successfully, if you must know.'

'But you were worried?'

'Yes. I told you before. I wanted to come and find you, but Beth said . . . she said you often went off, and you'd come back. And I didn't know where to start looking, in any case.'

He *wants* to know I was worried. It's as if he wants to push things to the limit, to test people. Me.

'Theo?' I say. 'It's not fair, making people worry just for the sake of it, to prove something. It's a cruel thing to do.'

He's silent.

I turn away, wriggle further down into the sleeping bag and pull the hood up to cover my face. I don't like him looking down at me like that, watching me.

Eventually he goes back into his room. He leaves the door open. It isn't very long before I hear the slow, rhythmic breathing of someone deeply asleep.

Gradually, I calm down.

I so wanted to believe that somehow I could save Theo from himself, just by being normal and loving. By understanding what it's like to feel sad, and to miss someone who's died. I could offer him that, at least. That's what I thought. But it's not enough, I realise now.

Everything seems different by the morning. I wake, late, to a strange, pale light. I crawl along the mattress and pull back the curtain on the little window next to the roof beam.

'Theo! Come and look! It's snowing!'

Theo groans. 'I'm asleep! You're too loud!'

'No, come here and see. It's amazing! Proper snow that's settling.'

He wakes up fully after a while; he wraps himself in his duvet and joins me at the window. 'You're cold!' he says. He holds out one edge of the duvet so I can cuddle in next to him, in the warm. He puts his arm round me and pulls me close. I'm acutely aware of his body, in a creased T-shirt and old pyjama bottoms, next to mine in my thin pyjamas. For a while, neither of us speaks. We watch the snow falling, piling on to the window ledge. It seems eerily quiet.

I sigh. 'I ought to phone Dad for a lift, before the snow gets too thick.'

'Why don't you stay?'

'I don't think so. Not after last night. You frightened me.'

'I promise I won't go off again,' Theo says. 'We'll have a good time. Really. I'd been drinking all day . . . too much, that's all it was. Sorry. I won't have any today.'

He seems so ordinary and sensible now that I start wondering what was real and what wasn't. That stuff about voices, the railway . . . did I imagine all that? Did I dream it?

I stare out of the window. The snow's falling fast, big soft feathery flakes. While I'm watching, the back door opens downstairs and Beth, Laura, Kit, Liu and Ellie spill out into the yard. They run in circles round the yard, and disappear through the gap in the wall into the garden. Their dark footprints are already filling up again with snow. I lean forward to open the window a little; icy air rushes in and with it, the sound of laughter, shrieking.

'Are you mad?' Theo says. 'It's freezing!' He pulls it shut again, sends a little pile of powdery snow over the ledge.

I laugh. 'I wanted to hear the snow. You know, that special soft sound it makes as it falls? Come on, let's get dressed and go outside with the others.'

It's funny the way snow transforms everything. Not just outside, where everything is cleaned and purified, all the dirt and muddle smoothed under a blanket of white, but people, too, are different. Even the adults.

Maddie's pulling on her boots and coat when we reach the kitchen. 'Have some breakfast,' she says. 'Then come on out.'

But we're too excited to stop for breakfast. Theo finds me some spare wellies and an old waxed jacket and we run out into the yard. Nick and Gabes are searching for some old plastic sledges in the barn. It's not deep enough yet for sledging, but it might be if the snow keeps going. The sky is so completely white, the air so still and cold, it really might.

We follow the prints round the side of the house to the orchard and the garden. The grass is already covered, except where people have scooped and rolled the snow to make snowmen. But they are not your average sort of snowmen with a small round head on a big round body; these are works of art, snow sculptures: a woman and a baby, no, two babies . . . and Kit's making a boy, and before long, with everyone working together, there'll be a whole snow family . . . Except that Gabes throws a snowball that hits Kit, and then another at Theo, and a big snowball fight breaks out instead.

I join in. I'm an expert, from years of experience with my brother.

'Ouch!' The bitter cold of wet snow down my neck makes me yell out.

Theo brushes the snow off, and kisses my neck to warm it up, but it tickles and makes me laugh. I run off again, and he chases after. Kit rugby-tackles me and brings me down in the snow. I'm a sprawling, laughing wreck, wet through.

I follow Maddie back in for coffee and toast.

In the warm kitchen Will, Beth's husband, is buttoning Phoebe and Erin into their winter coats, ready to take them into snow for their first time ever.

Beth hovers, anxious. She smiles at me. 'Your cheeks, Freya! Bright pink! Is it very cold?'

'Yes, but very fun too!' I say. 'I'm going out again as soon as I've phoned Dad and had some breakfast.'

'Come and help with the twins, if you want. We're going to the field the other side of the lane, where there's a gentle slope,' Will says, 'to try sledging.'

I'm shy with Will: I don't really know him yet, just the things I've heard from Beth, and it's awkward, knowing that he's made Beth unhappy. Right now, though, he seems nice.

Theo helps me pull off my boots. My toes are numb. Maddie pours the coffee. Everything is exactly as it should be.

'Can you stay a bit longer?' Maddie asks me, when she sees me getting my phone out. 'One of us can take you home later, to save your parents coming out in the snow.'

'Thanks. I'd like that.'

I go into the hall so I can talk more easily. Through the sitting-room doorway I can see Ellie with the kittens. She waves at me.

The phone rings for ages. Dad picks up eventually. 'Freya darling!' he says. 'Are you ready to come home? Have you had a good time?'

'I'm going to stay today, if that's OK by you. Maddie says they'll bring me home this evening. We're going sledging in a minute.'

'You must have more snow out there than we do. Here, it's just a light dusting,' Dad says. Mum calls out something. 'Hang on, your mother wants to wish you Happy Boxing Day!'

'Glad you've been having a good time, darling,' she says. Her voice sounds breathy, different to usual. 'We have too. A lovely long walk and a very romantic evening!'

'Well, that's good. You can tell me more when I see you later,' I say. 'Bye, Mum.'

Romantic? I can guess what that means. I needn't have felt guilty about not being with them for Christmas. It's obviously better that I wasn't there, that it was just the two of them . . .

But there's too much going on to be sad right now. Breakfast, and then sledging, for the whole afternoon.

I go back into the warm kitchen.

Theo keeps his promise. He's not moody, he doesn't drink, he doesn't go rushing off, or wind anyone up too much. Gabes is nice too. It's much easier being around them both with so many other people there. We join everyone in the sloping field above the stream, and take turns on the three sledges. At about three, before it starts getting dark, the grown-ups go off for a long walk, all except Nick, who's been called out to a farm in the next valley. Beth and Will take the twins back to the house to warm up, and Tom and Laura go with them, so it's just Theo, Gabes, Kit, Liu, Ellie and me left.

We trudge up the hill to a steeper slope, where the snow is still untouched, thick and deep and soft. It's stopped actually snowing, now; for a brief half-hour the sun comes out: a pale winter sun so low in the sky it throws pink shadows over the snow-covered fields, and then the pink turns to purple and blue. By four, it's almost dark.

We go down the slope in pairs on the sledges, shooting down the iced runs we've made over the afternoon. One girl and one boy on each sledge: I'm with Theo, and Kit with Liu, and Gabes takes Ellie. I go at the front, legs crunched up, with Theo behind, his legs stretched out either side of me, his arms tight round my waist. My ears are numb with cold; the air whizzes over my face, stinging it, as we go faster and faster. I can't stop myself squealing each time – Ellie and Liu are just the same – but the boys are silent and competitive: who can be fastest, stay on longest.

There's a magical moment each time we go down, when the sledge seems to fly over the snow, and the air rushes past; something to do with the cold, the silence that folds over the landscape, and just the whoosh of movement. I close my eyes and I could be anywhere, any time. It's even more spellbinding as the light fades and the first stars appear. The moon comes up, and the whole world turns silver. It's almost too beautiful to leave behind.

But we do. We're exhausted, and wet, and frozen to

the core. My face is raw with cold. Silent now, we walk back through the fields, through the dark that isn't properly dark because of the moonlit snow.

Whatever happens, I think, I will remember this perfect afternoon for ever.

Twenty-four

Maddie takes me home in the evening. She doesn't invite Theo to come too, or let him drive me. 'The roads will be icy,' she tells him when he objects. 'You've no experience with driving in snow. And I'm not taking any risks with Freya's safety.' Her voice sounds sharp.

She drives the van very slowly along the lane: someone's been along with a tractor, clearing a track, but even so, it's slippery. She has to concentrate, so we don't talk until she's turned on to the main road, nearer town. There's much less snow here.

'How did you think Theo was?' she says, out of the blue. 'Be truthful, Freya.'

I turn to look at her. She isn't smiling or anything.

'Beth told me about him disappearing off last night. I didn't realise at the time,' Maddie says. 'I'm sorry you were anxious about him.'

I don't know what to say. I don't want to betray Theo, but maybe . . . maybe his mum should know what he was like.

'I think he had too much to drink,' I say, tentatively.

'Yes. And did he talk to you? When he came back?'

'He was very tired. He'd been walking, in the cold . . .'

'Did he tell you where he went?'

I'm cold. A bit shaky. 'He said he went to see if the stream was frozen . . .' I look at her face, and I know I have got to tell her everything. I owe her that. 'And then he walked all the way to the railway line. He said it was because *she* told him to. That girl who died.'

'Bridie.' She says it matter-of-factly, as if she's not surprised by any of this. 'You know about her, of course.'

'Yes.' I wonder if she knows about me being on the train: that shocking, random event which catapulted me right into the centre of this family. But that isn't what's relevant right now. 'He says he hears Bridie's voice sometimes, telling him to do things.'

Maddie changes gear as we come down the hill to the roundabout under the railway bridge. She waits for the queue of snow-covered cars at the junction and then joins the line of traffic into the right lane and along the bypass. The snow here has already turned to brown slush.

'That's not so good,' Maddie says. 'I didn't know he was back there, again, in that state. I'm sorry to have to say this to you, Freya, about my own son. He got too involved with Bridie before she died. And she was very, very sick. Obviously, seeing what she did. It messed his head up, rather. He needs lots of help, to get over it.'

I stare out of the window. All the magical feeling I had before is trickling away. 'Help?' I say, blankly.

‘Professional help. He was seeing a counsellor in Oxford for a while, to help him get over Bridie’s death. I’ll have to set up some more sessions for him.’ Her voice brightens up a bit. ‘Of course he needs love and friendship, too: the usual things that make a difference to all of us.’ She smiles at me. ‘You’ve been through such sad things yourself; I know you understand more than most girls your age would.’

We stop at the traffic lights. Maddie turns to look at me. She pats my hand.

I feel like crying, but I don’t. ‘What was wrong with Bridie, exactly?’ I ask her.

‘Bridie’s mother was an alcoholic. Bridie was born with something called *fetal alcohol syndrome*. It affects the baby’s brain, means it doesn’t develop properly. And that’s probably why she got addicted herself, later, to drink and drugs . . . which made her mental condition . . . her depression . . . much worse. That’s on top of all the early neglect Bridie suffered. Her mother couldn’t love her properly, or even do the basic care a small child needs. Bridie ended up being fostered, but that wasn’t straightforward either. We tried to help. I did, for a while.’ Maddie’s voice falters. ‘I’m afraid I failed her miserably.’

My head’s starting to ache. I just want to get home, now.

‘Theo was obsessed with her. She was beautiful, in her thin scary way, I suppose. And she could be very exciting, with her sense of adventure, for someone like Theo who likes to push things to the limit, too.’

‘What do you mean?’ I ask.

'You know the way Theo wants to *experience* everything deeply? He can't bear the idea of a safe life – being comfortable. Not like most of us.'

'But today he was fine,' I say. 'So perhaps he just shouldn't drink. Today he was normal and lovely.'

I don't feel good, talking about him with his mother behind his back like this. I know Theo would hate it.

We're crawling along the London Road, in a long slow queue of cars.

'I think it's best you understand exactly what Theo's struggling with,' Maddie says. 'You're very young, Freya, to get mixed up in these things. I'm not sure it's what you need right now.'

I say goodbye politely when she stops the car, and thank her for having me for Christmas, but inside I'm seething. How dare she think she knows what I *need*!

I walk down our steep hill: the snow's settled here: it's strangely quiet with no traffic moving.

'You look wiped out!' Mum says when I finally get in and flop down at the supper table. 'I'll run you a bath when you've eaten something. You can join us for a film on the telly afterwards.'

'I think I'll just go up to bed,' I say. 'Thanks, Mum.'

My phone bleeps while I'm in the bath. I've left it in the bedroom, so can't check who it is. Maddie's worried face comes into my head. She was warning me, wasn't she? Just like Gabes, and Beth, and everyone. They all think they know best.

I dry myself on a new towel and pad along the landing to my bedroom.

It's a text from Miranda. At last! Heart beating fast, I open the message.

Hi Freya! Thank u for yr card. Want 2 meet me 2morrow?

It's such a relief I actually start to cry.

Yes! Where? I text back.

Yours? 11ish? Mx

:) F xx

Twenty-five

She arrives on the dot. I skip down the stairs to open the door before Mum gets there. We hug each other as if nothing has ever happened.

Mum waves to Miranda from the kitchen. 'Coffee, Miranda? Lovely to see you. Had a nice Christmas?'

'Yes thanks!' Miranda calls back. She looks at me. 'Shall we take our coffees upstairs?' she whispers. 'Or would that be really rude?'

'We can't talk down here,' I say. 'And Mum won't mind. She's got stuff to do anyway.'

Up in my room, sipping her mug of coffee, Miranda goes round looking at everything, the way she does. She picks up the Advent calendar from my bookshelf. 'Wow! This is amazing!'

'Danny made it.'

'Danny? You didn't tell me he was arty like that!'

'I didn't know. He's never told me. I mean, there was no reason to . . .'

'Well! Fancy that!' Miranda grins. 'So, what does this mean, Freya?'

'Nothing! Just Danny being sweet. *Dan*, I should say. That's what he calls himself now.'

'Hmm.' Miranda gives me one of her looks. 'Anyway, before we get on to Danny, first you've got to tell me what happened with Gabes.' Miranda settles down on my bed, back against the wall, just like the old days.

I think how to begin. 'It was difficult at first, of course. We talked in the café that time you saw us –' I glance at her – 'when you weren't speaking to me. He was . . . disappointed, I think. He seemed more cross with Theo than me. It was dead embarrassing. I felt terrible, for lying to him. And then we met again to talk properly about it, and Gabes was really nice. Generous. He was lovely at Christmas. That's where I've been the last two days: at Home Farm. Theo was there too. Gabes really isn't upset or anything now. We're still friends.'

'Really?'

'Yes. Honestly.'

She sighs. 'He's not like most blokes, then.'

'No. He isn't. That's one reason why I like him. And Theo isn't, either. That whole family . . . I've never met a family like them.'

Miranda sits forward on the bed. 'I don't get it, the way you are so under their spell. You've got your own amazing family, Freya, if only you'd wake up and see it.' She sighs. 'I could shake you, sometimes!'

I look at her, surprised. I don't answer her.

'Well, I'm glad it all turned out OK in the end,'

Miranda says. 'Maybe I was wrong about Gabes. None of it's worth us falling out over, anyway. I'm sorry I went off on one like I did.'

'I missed you loads,' I say.

'Really?'

'Of course. And I didn't understand why you were *so* mad with me.'

Miranda bites her lip. 'No? Couldn't you see that you being so secretive – lying to me, even – how that would make me feel? Like, shut out. Not wanted. As if you didn't trust me to understand.'

'I'm sorry,' I say. 'I was too mixed up myself. I was all in a muddle. I felt bad, really. I thought you'd tell me off. I don't know . . .'

'Which is why you should have talked about it all with me, Freya. Talking about things always makes them better. Isn't that what friends are for?'

'Yes. I guess.' We're both quiet for a bit. Then I say, 'So, what have you been doing?'

Miranda shrugs. 'Not much. Usual things. Been to the cinema a couple of times. I went to Tabby's party on Christmas Eve.'

'She didn't invite me.'

'No. Well, that was probably my fault. Sorry. I was still mad with you.'

We're both silent, awkward.

'What are you doing for New Year's Eve?' Miranda says.

'I'm not sure. I got invited to a party but it's in Birmingham, and Mum and Dad will never let me go. Not that I've asked.'

'You've changed,' Miranda says. 'You've got all these new friends.'

'Not really,' I say. 'Duncan – who's having the party – is Theo's friend, not mine. And they are all older than me, and that's a bit weird. And they are into drinking and smoking and being *clever* – the ones I've met, anyway. I don't really fit in. I'm not sure I even *want* to go.'

'So, you and Theo . . . are you actually going out together? Like, officially?'

'No. Well. I mean, I like him, and he likes me, I think, but there's lots of things that aren't right.'

'Like what?'

'He's a bit of a mess . . . Well, more than a bit, actually. It's all much too complicated.'

'Things with you always are!' Miranda laughs. 'Oh, Freya!'

It's good to be laughing together again. We make more coffee, and we eat the biscuits Mum's left out for us on the kitchen table.

Miranda wants to see the new pieces in my art portfolio, and it begins to feel easier between us again. She flips through the pictures I've mounted on card for my project. 'I love this one of the beach, with the torn-up bits of photograph. You definitely should do Art at college.'

'I don't know,' I say. 'I don't want to just do one thing. I like learning about everything. I want to go places and find out more about me, who I am, who I might be. I want my life to be bigger, somehow. To mean something.'

Miranda wrinkles up her nose. 'Don't start getting all serious and deep and philosophical now. Please, Freya?'

It's not the right time to tell Miranda about Theo's problems, about Bridie and all that. Instead, I tell her the happy things: the Christmas meal and sledging.

Mum calls up. 'Do you two want lunch?'

'Do we?' I ask Miranda.

'Of course!'

We trek back downstairs. Mum's made tomato and basil soup.

Miranda knows exactly how to win over my parents. She tells Mum how amazing her cooking is, and gushes about our house to Dad, which makes him feel good. I notice how it tips the balance back, having a fourth person at the kitchen table again. We're a bit more like a family with Miranda chatting and Mum asking questions and Dad flirting a bit: he can't help himself when Miranda is so bright and gorgeous.

Late afternoon, after Miranda's gone home, Dad calls up to me in my room. 'Come and watch a film with us, Freya!'

Mum's making tea in the kitchen. She looks up as I come into the sitting room. 'Home-made Christmas cake? Or a slice of stollen?'

'You made a cake?'

'Don't sound so shocked, Freya!'

'I didn't know, that's all. I didn't think you'd done any Christmas cooking.'

This is the first time she's made a Christmas cake

since Joe died. I join her in the kitchen to have a proper look. She's iced it and everything. Glossy white, with peaks like snow.

'Do you want to put the decorations on it?' She points to the small grey cardboard box on the table.

My heart gives a lurch. I'd almost forgotten about them. I open the lid. Inside, nestled in tissue paper, are the little china decorations that Evie gave us when Joe and I were small: a seal, a polar bear, a penguin and an Arctic fox. Every year, we'd put them on the Christmas cake.

'They might need a dust!' Mum says.

I wipe each one carefully with a tea towel and arrange them on the cake. I find two little fir trees in the box too, totally out of scale, and a robin. I put them all on to make a little winter scene.

Mum laughs. 'I don't think it will pass Dad's *good taste* test!'

He's lit the wood-burning stove in the sitting room. It changes the light in the room: makes everything softer and more cosy. We sit together on the cream sofa, me in the middle, and for once Mum doesn't fuss about plates and crumbs.

'It's a long time since we've done this!' Dad says. 'Much too long.'

'Freya's got her own life, these days,' Mum says. 'She doesn't want to hang around with her boring old parents!'

'That's *so* not true,' I say. 'It's not like that at all. You're hardly ever here. You're always too busy.'

She looks genuinely surprised, as if she hasn't even thought of that before.

‘Ready then? I’m pressing Start,’ Dad says. He leans back, and slips his arm round my shoulders. I snuggle into him. It’s ages since I’ve done that, too.

We watch the film.

Mum cuts more cake.

She kicks off her shoes and curls up, her feet in my lap. It’s cosy, snuggling together like this. It seems ages since we were so close. I’d forgotten how safe and good it makes me feel.

‘There are a few more presents that we haven’t opened,’ Dad says when the film’s finished. He reaches over the end of the sofa and fishes up two parcels.

The one from Evie and Gramps is for me. There’s a note inside in careful copperplate handwriting, and a ferry ticket.

‘For my next visit. Look!’

‘Nice one,’ Dad says. ‘Good old Gramps.’

I pull out a small package wrapped in turquoise tissue paper and tied with silver string. Inside is a new sketchbook, hand-made, with a deep blue marbled cover and thick cream paper with bits of leaf and petal pressed into the fibre.

‘How lovely,’ Mum says. ‘Isn’t Evie clever?’

The other parcel is the one from me to Mum and Dad, which they’ve saved for today so I can see them open it. They unwrap it together, giggling and silly. I’m suddenly nervous in case they don’t like it.

But they do. For a moment I think they might even cry.

It’s the small square watercolour painting of Beady

Pool. Just sand, and sea, and the curve of the rocky bay, in bright sunlight under a blue summer sky. The frame is bleached wood, like driftwood.

'It's so beautiful,' Mum says. 'It's to treasure for ever.'

'It's a happy painting,' Dad says. 'Full of light and love. Thank you.'

Mum comes upstairs after I've had my bath; she taps lightly on my bedroom door. 'Can I come in, Freya?'

'Yes. I'm in bed. But it's fine.'

She comes in and sits down on the edge of my bed. She sighs. 'It seems I keep on getting it wrong.'

'What do you mean?'

'Something you said downstairs, about us always being busy.'

'You are. It's the truth. I know I'm busy too and going out more these days, but you and Dad are hardly ever here. That's why we hardly do anything together any more.' I'm surprised how sad it makes me feel, saying this out loud.

'I didn't realise,' Mum says. 'I thought you didn't want to. I thought it was all part of you growing up and not needing us any more. I was doing my best to give you some space. My own mother was so useless at that.' She looks miserable.

I don't say anything. I don't know where to begin. So many things I could tell her, if I could only start.

Mum leans over and kisses the top of my head. 'Sweet sixteen,' she says, wistfully. 'Almost grown up.'

'Not really,' I say. 'It doesn't feel like that to me.'

And then the words begin to come, and I start to tell her, about Gabes, and Theo, and Bridie, and me and everything.

All of it comes tumbling out.

Afterwards, she looks shocked. Stunned into silence.

I wait.

'It's a lot to take in,' she says eventually. 'I'm so sad you couldn't tell me before. And I'm so, so pleased you have now, Freya. Everything makes much more sense to me now.'

'Really?' I say. Tears come into my eyes. I can't stop them.

'Oh, Freya!' Mum holds me in her arms and lets me cry. She wipes my face with a tissue and smooths my hair. She smiles at me. 'You've brought it all back to me so vividly, what it was like for me being sixteen, seventeen. First loves, the terrible complications! And how exciting it all is, too. Life opening out, and all the different possibilities!'

'It was like that for you, too?'

'Yes! I think it's how it's meant to be, Freya, when you're sixteen.' She laughs, softly. 'Can I tell some of this to Dad? Do you mind? I think it would help him too.'

'Not everything. Just tell him a bit,' I say.

'The edited highlights.'

'Yes.'

'Not anything that will make him worry too much.'

'Exactly.'

'And you mustn't worry either, Mum.' I yawn, exhausted.

'No. I'll do my best. Though *worrying* is a mother's prerogative. Part of the job description, I'm afraid!' She kisses me. 'Please, please try to talk to me when you're anxious about things in future. Tell me what's going on. I will always make time to listen to you, Freya. Even when I *am* busy.' She stands up. 'But right now I'll leave you to get your beauty sleep!'

She stops at the doorway to look back at me. 'Sweet dreams, Freya. My dearest, darling daughter!'

After she's gone, I snuggle down under the duvet. I am really sleepy, now, but there's a kind of lightness inside me, a sense that something has lifted at last.

Twenty-six

To begin with, I was bowled over by Gabes' family, by all the life and love I found in that beautiful house with its wild garden tucked into the bottom of the hidden valley among the woods and fields. It was just like falling in love. I *so* wanted to belong to them all, to feel safe and loved and surrounded too. And falling for Gabes and Theo was all part of that.

When you fall in love, Mum says, sometimes you see everything through a bit of a golden haze. Or you choose what to see, and what to ignore. I think that's what I did. It's more obvious to me now that Gabes and Theo and Beth – the whole family, probably – have got their own problems and struggles and secrets too. Of course they have. They aren't any more perfect than my own family.

And I *do* have a family of my own.

Even though it's small.

Even without my brother, Joe.

There's still Dad and Mum and me, Evie and Gramps. And they love me. I *can* tell them stuff. I don't have to be quite so secretive, or pretend I don't need them, when really I do.

I think about all this as I lie in bed, listening to the sounds of a normal Saturday morning drifting upstairs. Voices; Radio 4; the clink of cups on the kitchen table.

I've decided something else important, too. Miranda was right: talking about things did help.

I thought I could make Theo better, but I can't. And while he's so messed up, so *not well*, I'll be his friend but I don't want to be anything more than that. He's too unpredictable. Too caught up with himself.

As Theo's *friend*, there's something I still want to do for him. I know Gabes was doubtful about it, and he might be right. Maybe it won't help Theo much, but I'm going to try. I phone him to say I want us to go on a secret trip, but we'll need transport, so can he borrow Maddie's van? Or Beth's car? For a whole day, starting early? And he says yes.

Theo collects me from our house on Sunday morning in Beth's car, so Mum and Dad get to meet him very briefly. Everyone's on best behaviour. Theo does his posh Oxford voice. Dad goes on a bit too much about *safe driving*, and *taking breaks*, and *absolutely nothing to drink*. But they let me go.

I don't tell Theo exactly where we're going until we've started driving. I've got the map on my knees. I give him directions to the M4.

Theo swears as a lorry in front slows to go up the hill. He doesn't like overtaking. He'd hoped to drive the whole way in the slow lane. He's *so* not the reckless driver.

'Where next?' he says. He changes down a gear.

'We just keep going, 'I say, 'across the bridge into Wales.'

He frowns. 'Freya, this is all a bit mad.'

'Trust me,' I say. I've got the road map open on my knees. I've worked it all out. I trace the roads with my finger. 'M4 to Swansea, then it's smaller roads, all the way to the Gower coast. We're going to the beach in your story.'

Theo goes very quiet.

'Bridie's beach,' I say, firmly. 'The one she wanted to go to because she went there once when she was little and it was a happy place for her.'

'I know what beach,' Theo says.

'Did you go there for real, ever, with Bridie?'

'No.'

'But she wanted to go there with you, right? It was special for her?'

'Yes.' Theo sucks in his breath. He's concentrating on driving.

I keep going, regardless. 'I thought, if we went to that beach and you thought about Bridie there and remembered her and we did some sort of ceremony – like lighting a fire for her, or making something out of driftwood, or . . . I don't know . . . writing a poem in the sand – maybe it would help you to say goodbye. And then the voices might stop.'

The road surface changes and the tyres sound extra noisy. The motorway is busy, people going home, going on holidays, visiting friends . . . the whole world on the move for the New Year.

Theo stays silent. But he keeps on driving westwards.

Inside the car's getting hot and stuffy. I turn the dial on the fan to waft some air on my face. The landscape flashes past, a blur of fields and hedges and trees, the odd building.

I just pray it works out; it will all be my fault if it doesn't. But to me it seems exactly the right thing to do. Theo can start the New Year with a new feeling. It'll be a proper fresh start.

The bridge is just ahead now. There's more sky, somehow: air and light and a different smell.

Now we're through the toll and into Wales, Theo seems to catch my mood. 'Put some music on,' he says. 'Beth's CDs are in there.'

I open the glove compartment and flip through her CD case. I look for the song she played for me that time she gave me a lift back home, but I can only remember fragments of the lyrics, not the title or even the band. I find an album I recognise; it's got this amazing song on it that Mum used to play all the time.

Go, Leave . . . Listening to it now, it seems strangely appropriate for Theo. It suddenly dawns on me why Mum played it so much. It's a song about letting go of someone you love, even though your heart is aching. The words are sad and beautiful.

The road stretches out in front of us, a long grey ribbon.

As we get past Newport and Cardiff, the landscape

changes again. Hills. Forest. Rows of houses. More hills. The sky is grey: at one point it starts to snow, small, hard icy flakes. It stops again. The sky clears.

It takes longer than I expected. Two hours before we're off the motorway and on to smaller roads. It gets harder to read the map. Theo stops the car in a layby so he can look too: he shows me the beach we are aiming for. He's been to Wales before, but to me the place names are all strange, unfamiliar.

At last we turn off the main road and bump down a track, and Theo parks the car. We're both stiff from sitting still.

'Here we are, then,' Theo says. 'Bridie's beach.'

It's a long walk down the cliff to the beach. We run the last bit once it flattens out: it's a river estuary, and at low tide the beach is a vast stretch of sand with the river winding through the middle, dividing it into two, with stepping stones across, exactly like in Theo's story. It's exhilarating to be able to run in the fresh air after being cooped up so long. We race each other, laughing and shouting – impossible to hear as the wind snatches our voices and whisks them away to nothing. There are miles of empty sand, a few birds, no people at all.

Theo grabs my hand and we run together down to the water's edge. The sea is wild, stormy. Waves roll in, a constant line of breakers, spreading out into lace over the ridged sand. The air is damp with spray, Theo's hair covered in a mass of tiny water droplets; even his eyebrows and eyelashes are beaded with it.

We break apart and run again parallel to the sea,

dodging the waves as they break and spread out and send foaming water further up the sand.

'I think the tide's coming in,' I say, but Theo doesn't hear.

The wind and the spray scour my face, cold and clean. I smooth my wet hair out of my stinging eyes. I turn my back to the wind and begin walking up the huge beach, searching for stones, for polished sea glass and other magic. Further along there are three jagged rocks, and a deep pool, and then, as I keep walking, I find you can get round to another, smaller sandy beach, more sheltered from the wind. I beckon Theo over.

He follows me round the rocks.

At the top of this beach the cliff rises sharply, not like the way we came down on the other beach where the river has carved a wide valley.

Theo points up. 'Look!'

'What?'

'See there? That dark space beneath the overhanging rock? That's the cave!'

I'm not sure I want to go clambering so high up; for now, I'm trying to think what we should do to say a final goodbye to Bridie.

There's loads of wood that's been washed up by storms. I start collecting it, piling it up to help it dry out more so we can have a fire later, if we want. Theo's a small dark speck at the far end of the beach now. I try to remember what he wrote in his story – they made a fire, didn't they? And they planned to swim in the moonlight . . . only the tide was too high . . .

When I next look for him, I can't see Theo anywhere. I scan the beach. No sign of him. Surely he wouldn't think of trying to swim? Not in such rough sea? You would drown in an instant. I turn around again to the cliff. I screw my eyes up to see better. The light is too bright, but there's something – someone – moving along towards the ledge about halfway up. Now I know he's safe – sort of – I go back to collecting firewood. There are beautiful shells too: I line them up in a row. I rearrange them to make the shapes of the letters for Bridie's name, collect some more. I stand back, so I can see how they'd look from Theo's viewpoint on the cliff, but I guess they're too small for him to see from up there. I pick up some bigger stones to make a fireplace. I wish I'd packed proper food for cooking on a fire.

I go searching for more treasures. The tide's definitely coming in; it's already much closer than I expected. I start to run towards the sea; I know Theo's still up on the cliff, but I run anyway, down to the edge of the rocks we walked round earlier, to check we can still get back round to the main part of the beach.

But it's already too late. I'm so mad with myself I could cry. Such a stupid, stupid mistake to make! How could I? Me, Freya, who's always so careful about tides! It's been bred into me from when I was born, practically; all those island summers with Evie and Gramps, the thousands of time they've drummed it into me . . .

The sea is already deep and crashing on to the rocks. There is no possible way we can wade back round now.

The sandy beach is so flat and wide that the sea comes in really fast. On parts of the Brittany coast the tide is faster than a galloping horse. I know that, but I don't know this beach, on this part of Wales. I start to run back up the sand, calling and waving to Theo. The wind is strong, it whips the sound away, he can't hear me, he's too busy exploring to notice what is happening down here. There is no other way off the beach now except up.

I try to calm myself down. There's no immediate panic. I've got time to slow down a bit, to find a good route up the cliff. If Theo managed, I can too. And maybe the sea won't come up the whole beach in any case: there's a tide-line, after all. I noticed because I made sure to put the driftwood above that mark, on the drier sand.

I try to remember what the moon is doing: if I were on St Ailla I'd *know* instantly! I'd have been paying attention to all that. The full moon and the new moon are the strong spring tides, with the biggest reach.

Theo's waving and pointing at something. I can't hear what he's shouting, but I guess he's just noticed the sea too, how far up it has come. I'm trying to think. The moon was out when we were sledging. Boxing Day. It was about three-quarters then. So that means it will be full moon either tonight or tomorrow. The highest tide.

I watch Theo make his way down the cliff. He makes it look easy. He jumps the last bit. 'We're cut off,' he said.

'Yes.'

'That's exciting!' he says. 'We'll have to stay here, then.'

'At least as long as it takes the tide to come the rest of the way up and then down again, till it clears the rocks. Theo, it might be hours! It'll be dark!'

'Or we could go up the cliff? I've been about half-way, to that cave, and you can probably go further up and over the top, and I expect we can find a way back that way.' He grins at me.

I'm staring at the smooth cliff face above the ledge: there's no obvious way up that I can see from here.

'Or we could stay in the cave,' Theo says.

'How big is it? Is it damp?'

'It's big enough. We could make a fire up there. It would warm up, I reckon. We'd be fine.' Theo's eyes are glittery bright.

'OK,' I say, 'Let's lug the wood up there. You might have to help me a bit. I don't like heights.'

He doesn't tease me, or get exasperated about how slow I am, picking my way over the rocks. I need both hands in places, so he ends up carrying the wood and I just focus on clinging on. Below us, the sea rushes in, grey and swirling and wild. Once I'm up on the ledge, shaky but safe, I dare to look down. The sand's almost completely covered. My shell letters have already been washed away.

Theo makes three trips to bring up all the wood, just in time.

He fishes a box of matches from his jeans pocket.

'What else have you got that's useful?' I ask.

'Da – dah!' He magics a bar of chocolate from his coat pocket. 'Emergency rations.'

It takes a while to coax a small fire; the wood's

damp, it smoulders and stutters but eventually we get it going enough to make a little warmth if we sit right close to it, and the cave does keep the wind off a bit.

I shiver.

Theo huddles up close behind me, so I'm sitting with my back leaning into him. He unbuttons his coat so he can wrap it half round me, too. He rests his chin on my head.

My hands are still freezing; I slip my right one into Theo's coat pocket and curl it round for warmth. My fingers touch something small and cool and metallic: I pull it out of the pocket and hold it out on the palm of my hand to see. The light from the fire catches the gold surface and makes it gleam. It's a small ring, like a wedding band.

I pull away from Theo slightly. 'Where did you get this?'

He leans forward to see. 'What?'

'This ring.' But I know the answer even before he says the words.

'Bridie gave it to me. The last time I saw her. She wanted me to have it. I didn't want it, but she insisted I take it. "It's worth something, it's real gold," she said, even though it isn't.' He takes it from the palm of my hand and turns it round in his own. It's too tiny to fit over any of his fingers.

Get rid of it, I want to say. *Let the ring go, and let go of Bridie too.* But I know that won't work. He's got to decide for himself. You can't make someone do that.

He reaches forward and lays the ring down on the flat stone near the entrance of the cave. He starts telling me about some human bones that were found in a cave near here, along with mammoth bones, and the bones of a horse and a dog. 'The man who found her called her The Red Lady; he thought she was from Roman times. Only she turned out to be a man, and way, way older that that: from Palaeolithic times. Don't you think that's extraordinary?' he says. 'There were people here twenty-six thousand years ago!'

'What do you think they were like?'

'Same as us, I reckon. Thinking about the same sort of things: getting enough food to eat. Keeping warm. Falling in love. Being happy.'

I laugh. 'And the meaning of life and everything!'

'I'm serious,' he says. 'Don't joke about it.'

'You're *too* serious, Theo,' I say. But I regret it, instantly, because that's what we're supposed to be here for, after all. The serious business of saying goodbye to Bridie.

I make my mind travel back, all the weeks and months to that train journey, the moment of impact, and everything that followed. I'd wanted to know who it was, and why. And now I have most of my answers. I know it was Bridie, that she was ill, her mind addled by drink, drugs, stuff that messes you up really badly. She took her own life when she was in a state where she couldn't think clearly.

'When was the last time you saw Bridie?' I ask Theo. 'Tell me about it.'

He sighs. I feel it shudder through his whole body. He rests his chin on my head. I notice, suddenly, how dark it's getting in the cave, the light outside fading to grey. But it's easier to talk in the dark like this.

'We had a drink in a café,' Theo says. 'But we couldn't stay long: she was shaking, she couldn't speak properly. She said she was scared all the time.

'So we went outside. I had this stupid idea that she'd feel better in the open air, in the sunshine. I held her arm and led her down the steps to the river and we sat on a bench for a while and watched the light on the water. She told me she'd lost herself. That nothing gave her any joy. All she wanted to do was sleep.'

Theo's shaking too, just remembering. 'She'd never talked to me like that before. And nothing I said made the slightest difference. She'd sort of gone, already.'

'That's the illness,' I say. 'She was really ill, Theo.'

'It was still a shock,' Theo says, 'to hear how she died. Unbearable, really.'

There's nothing I can say to make it better.

'So, I guess it was a choice,' he says. 'She decided she'd had enough. But it's terrible for everyone else.'

'Her family?'

'What family? She didn't have one. Her mum was already dead. She never knew her dad. We were the closest thing to a family she ever had. And we were rubbish.'

'Well, I think she was lucky to have had you as a friend, Theo.'

'But I wasn't enough. Nowhere near.'

We stop talking. We sit in the grey light of a winter sunset when there is no sun, just the steady draining of light.

'OK,' Theo says at last. 'Now what? What do I do? I haven't a clue.'

'Think of a happy time,' I say. 'A good memory of Bridie, like when she was little, and you played together. Think of her laughing, and full of life. And say goodbye.'

He walks out on to the windy ledge. I hate him standing so close to the cliff edge like that. The tide must be at the highest point: the sea's bashing the bottom of the cliff now, crashing and thundering as the waves break on to the rock face and send up great plumes of spindrift.

I watch as he lifts his arms up: a dark figure, silhouetted against the grey sky. He hurls something with one hand, and for the briefest moment I think I catch the flicker of light on gold.

I glance down at the stone. The ring has gone. He must have picked it up as he left the cave and I didn't notice. He picked it up and he let it go.

And I'm glad, glad, glad.

Now there's just the long, cold wait for the tide to turn and the sea to retreat down the sand, and we will at last be able to start walking back to the car, and travel home in the dark. And it will be the end of the old year, the beginning of the new.

Twenty-seven

It's properly dark by the time the tide's gone down enough for us to walk back the beach way to the car. We're both shivering with cold. I remember to text Mum to say we're fine and I'm going to be late, and not to worry.

We sit in the car to eat the sandwiches I'd packed.

'Are you too tired to drive?' I ask.

Theo shakes his head. 'We can stop for coffee, any way. It'll be fine. At least it's not snowing.'

The roads have emptied out compared to the morning. We listen to Beth's entire CD collection (all five discs) and sing along to the radio. We stop for petrol and coffee at the service station.

'You've missed Duncan's party, now,' I say. 'Do you mind?'

'No.' Theo laughs. 'It'll be a bit of a piss up, and I've promised Mum to give up drinking for now. And I'll see Duncan in a couple of weeks anyway when the term starts.'

We drive along in silence for a while. I'm trying to summon up courage to tell Theo what I've decided.

'I don't think I can visit you in Oxford this term,' I say, carefully. 'I think it's better that way.'

Theo doesn't say anything. The turn-off for our junction off the motorway is coming up soon. When we wait at the lights before the roundabout, he turns to look at me. 'This is the *let's just be friends* conversation, yes?'

'Yes.'

Theo sighs. 'What did Gabes say? Or was it my mother?'

'It's nothing to do with Gabes, or Maddie,' I say. 'It's about me. About what's right for me.'

Theo doesn't reply. But he nods his head slightly, as if he accepts what I have said.

We're almost home. I can see the lights of the city in the sweep of the valley; the orange glow lighting up the night sky.

'*All will be well,*' Theo says. '*All will be well. And all manner of things will be well.*'

'What's that from?'

'Guess.'

'The Bible?'

'No. Lady Julian of Norwich.'

'*Who?*'

'Medieval mystic. 1342 to 1416.'

'Honestly, Theo! What are you like!'

'Impressively well read? An inspiration?'

'If you weren't driving I'd hit you!'

Theo laughs.

I'm relieved. It is all going to be all right. We will still be friends. I'll still be able to visit Home Farm sometimes. And in just a few hours, it will be the first day of the New Year, a new beginning for us all.

Twenty-eight

Beginnings, endings. One door shuts and another door opens. That's what Evie said to me, way back at the end of the summer.

I'm sitting on my bed, making a bracelet for Miranda out of different coloured silk threads. I've chosen the colours I associate with her: apricot, cream, orange, pink, purple and apple green. It's a new, complicated chevron pattern with six strands so I have to concentrate and be very patient, methodically weaving and knotting the coloured threads, but it's satisfying, too: the rhythm of it. After a while my hands learn the pattern; my fingers move by instinct.

I start thinking about my own life, with its different coloured strands, like a bracelet. I imagine saying that to Miranda and making her hoot with laughter. The different strands weave in and out of each other, so that one colour is sometimes stronger or more vivid than the others. Sometimes there seems to be just one dominant colour, and no tones or shades. If you look really closely, though, you can see that the other more subtle colours are still there. Gabes' strand is gold, and Theo's a darker colour, not black but blue-dark, like a night sky.

There's another thread that has been there all along, running underneath, though I've only just started to notice it. Danny. And I'm not sure yet what colour he'll be; it's too soon to tell. Turquoise blue, like a summer sea? Or silver, like a live mackerel? Or something else, quite unexpected?

The post arrives. Mum comes upstairs and knocks on my door. 'Postcard for you, from Evie.' She hands it to me.

'Thanks, Mum.' I wait for her to go back downstairs before I read it.

Evie says she loves the painting I sent them for Christmas. They are going to frame it and hang it in the sitting room in pride of place above the fireplace. Gramps sends his love too. *Guess what? The old lighthouse buildings have been sold! Or maybe you've heard already? Danny's dad was over here just before Christmas.*

I stare at the words. Does she mean what I think she means? That Danny's family are buying the lighthouse buildings?

Years ago, Joe and I sunbathed in the overgrown garden next to the empty buildings and imagined living there. We talked about having special curved furniture to fit in the round rooms in the old tower. The view from the top would be amazing.

Two and a half years ago, when the derelict

buildings were actually for sale, I wanted Dad to buy them and do them up so we could have our own house on St Ailla and live there all year round. It was after we'd sold the big house near the canal; Mum and Dad were looking for somewhere new, to make a fresh start after Joe died. But Dad said no: Mum would never contemplate living there. Being so close to the sea would be a constant reminder of losing Joe. Dad had a whole string of other reasons, too. There's only one little shop; it's hundreds of miles away from their work and friends; it's a little too close to his mum and dad, lovely as they are. Island life is just too small. And I told him what Gramps always says: *if you want to see a lot, standing still in one place is a good way to do it.*

For a second, a pang of envy clutches my heart.

But I know it couldn't ever be mine, really. And if that's so, then there's no one I'd rather see living in the old lighthouse buildings than Danny and his family.

I send him a message.

What's this about the lighthouse????

Danny texts me almost straight back.

It's true! We've bought it. Going to do it up for summer holidays!

I'm so excited I have to talk to him. I call him. 'Danny? It's me!'

'Freya!'

'It's amazing news. Why didn't you tell me before?'

'It's only just happened. We had to wait for the bank to decide about a loan. We've got to borrow loads of money. We'll be broke for years. But Mum and Dad were determined . . . Hattie's over the moon!'

Hattie is Danny's little sister. 'She can have a bedroom in the tower,' I say. 'Like a princess!'

'It'll be years of work, first,' Danny says. 'Every hour of every holiday, probably. But I'm excited about it. It'll be awesome when it's finished.'

'I'll be going over to St Ailla in April,' I say. 'It was my Christmas present from Gramps. Will you all be there, then?'

'I guess.'

'So I'll see you then?'

'Yes.'

That's over three months' time. By then, I'll have finished my next project for Art. We're doing life drawing this term; I'm doing a special study of the human hand. Both Danny and I will have exams coming up; maybe we could do Biology revision together, in between his work on the lighthouse with his dad. Biology is Danny's favourite subject: he's going to be either a marine biologist or an oceanographer, he says.

I start to see it all unfold in my mind's eye.

First there's the journey. The train, then the ferry.

The sea will be rough, with a strong swell that makes the boat roll. A spring gale will be blowing. Everyone on the ferry will be feeling sick. But after four or five hours we'll be nearly there, and as soon as we get alongside the first of the outer islands at the edge of the archipelago the rolling will stop as the sea becomes more shallow. The mood on the boat will lift. I'll see a swallow: the first of the summer.

When we arrive at the harbour on Main Island I'll make my way down the stone steps to the little island ferry, *Spirit*, for the final leg of my journey.

Evie and Gramps will be waiting on the jetty at St Ailla to welcome me. Evie will have cooked something special for supper – her fish pie with prawns, perhaps, made with potatoes Gramps has grown in the garden, and redcurrant meringue cake. Gramps will open a bottle of best bitter for himself and pour a champagne flute of sparkling wine for Evie, and we will toast my arrival.

'The swallows are back,' I'll tell Gramps. 'I saw my first one today.'

Later, when Evie and I are alone together, she will ask me questions about life at home. About Mum and Dad. Miranda. College work. My paintings. I'll tell her about my new project.

'You can draw our hands,' Evie will say. 'Mine and Gramps'. That'll take you a while, with all those little wrinkle lines to sketch in!'

I'll tell her about Gabes and Theo and the family who caught me in their spell and swept me away.

'Don't be so dazzled by the moon and the stars that you stop seeing what's right under your feet!' Evie will say. I'll know she's thinking about her and Gramps; they were childhood sweethearts but she went away from home and it was only many years later she found him again.

'No need to be in such a rush about everything,

either,' Evie will say. 'Take your time. Friends, boyfriends: don't ever settle for less than the best.'

I'll laugh, and I'll say yes, I know that. I want a life that means something, that is big enough to make a difference. I want to be open to it all, and I want to go on learning new things.

'Whatever you do, wherever you go, you'll always be welcome here,' Evie will say. 'You and whoever you choose to bring with you, Freya, for whatever reason.'

And perhaps Gramps will hear our voices, talking softly, back and forth, in the sitting room. He'll come slowly downstairs to join us, one creaky step at a time.

Gramps will look lovingly at me, and then he'll turn to Evie.

'She's like the swallows,' Gramps will say, 'our Freya. Coming back to us each year. Bringing the summer with her.'

About the Author

Julia Green is the Course Leader on the MA in Writing for Young People at Bath Spa University, and has had three novels published by Puffin and three by Bloomsbury: *Breathing Underwater*, *Drawing with Light* and *Bringing the Summer*. She lives in Bath.

Learn more about Julia and her writing with a brief Q & A.

When you were Freya's age, what kind of books did you like to read?

When I was Freya's age, I was reading books for A level English: *King Lear* and *Measure for Measure* by Shakespeare; contemporary plays like *The Royal Hunt of the Sun* by Peter Shaffer; novels by Thomas Hardy (*Tess of the d'Urbervilles*, *Far from the Madding Crowd*) and D.H. Lawrence (*Sons and Lovers*). I read *Wuthering Heights* by Emily Brontë, Jane Eyre by Charlotte Brontë, and *Pride and Prejudice* (Jane Austen). I started reading the Romantic poets about this time (Keats, Wordsworth) and also poetry by Dylan Thomas, Stevie Smith, Philip Larkin, Ted Hughes and Seamus Heaney. I loved Dodie Smith's *I Capture the Castle*; *Catcher in the Rye* (J.D. Salinger), and historical romances by Georgette Heyer and Jean Plaidy . . . I read widely, everything I could get my hands on! My parents loved books and our house was full of them. I had a brilliant English teacher called Miss Fox, and

she suggested books to me too. We went to see a production of *The Tempest* by the RSC at Stratford-upon-Avon and I was blown away by how magical it was. I've never forgotten it. I use quotations from *The Tempest* in my novel *Breathing Underwater*.

When you are writing, to what extent do you draw on your own experiences?

All my stories are a mixture of 'real life', closely observed or remembered, and imagination. Different combinations of the real and the made-up. I do use my experiences a lot, but always re-imagined. Memories, thoughts and feelings are transformed in the writing of them. But that's not the same as saying my novels are autobiographical. They most definitely are not! My characters are not me. They are all imagined, created by me. But I need to feel a connection to the material I am writing.

How long does it take you to write a book?

Different novels take different amounts of time. I think and dream and imagine and write notes for a long while before I start writing down the story. Once I know enough to start typing on my laptop, it takes me about nine months to a year. *Breathing Underwater* took the longest: that's because I wrote one version then realised there was a better way to tell the story, with the parallel sections of 'This Summer' and 'Last Summer', and I rewrote the whole novel completely! I'm very proud of taking that time to get it right. I'm a slow writer because I think so much, and rewrite and edit a lot. Plus I'm not writing full-time: I have another job, as a university lecturer teaching Creative Writing.

What do you hope readers will take away from reading your books?

I hope my readers will immerse themselves in the story. I hope they will be able to 'see' the places I describe and imagine themselves there. I hope they will be moved and feel strong emotions alongside my characters, going on their own emotional journey. I hope they will think about things: their own lives, choices, friends, families, relationships. I hope they will put down the book at the end and feel satisfied and uplifted.

If you could recommend just one book for everyone to read what would it be?

Impossible question, but if you could only read one book, it would have to be a children's book: *Tom's Midnight Garden* by Philippa Pearce. Like the best children's books, it's a book for readers of any age. It's a beautiful and moving story. It's perfectly constructed, I think, and profound about the connections between the young and the old, between past and present, and the importance of memory.

Why I wrote Bringing the Summer

I am deeply attached to my character Freya, who I first wrote about in *Breathing Underwater*. I carried on thinking about her after the novel was published, even while writing *Drawing with Light*. My head was full of questions: what would it be like for Freya, two years later, as she becomes the age her brother was when he died? How would she feel now about her family, and being an 'only' child? I wanted to write about her family, but also other families. I also started thinking about the different ways people cope with the loss of someone they love so deeply, several years after the event. Some people seem to stay sad, or become bitter or depressed, but others find courage and embrace life and all it has to offer in a new way. I knew Freya would be like this. She'd see how precious life really is. She'd want her own life to have meaning and purpose.

Even though I am so drawn to the island where Freya spends the summers, this story is set mostly in the city where Freya lives with her parents. I've 'borrowed' some aspects of a place I know very well, but altered it in my imagination. Some chapters are set in Oxford: Theo is a student there. (I was too, a long time ago.)

Freya longs to be part of a bigger, happier family than her own. At sixteen, she's thinking about friendships, and boys, and making important choices of her own about the kind of person she is and the life she wants to lead. She makes some mistakes, too! All these aspects of growing up fascinate me. It's important to me that novels deal with real life in a way that allows readers to think – and be challenged, too, by uncomfortable or painful events as well as happier ones. I want my writing to be honest and truthful.

Gradually Freya's story began to emerge in my notebooks and I was ready to start work on the laptop. A dramatic incident on a train journey gave me a key scene for early in the novel, and led me towards a whole set of new characters: the big family that Freya becomes involved with. I wondered at first whether the incident was too painful, but I decided that I needed to be truthful about these things. 'Growing up' isn't always an easy time of life. And for some people life is unbearably hard, through no fault of their own. I hope I have balanced out the pain with moments of fun, happiness and hope. Ultimately, Freya is a person full of life and love and promise. She's like the swallows, who bring the summer with them.

My favourite section in Bringing the Summer

I love many scenes in this novel, including the chapters set in Oxford, the ones set on the beach on the Gower, in Wales, and the ending scene too. But I've chosen Chapter Six, when Freya first visits Gabes' house. I loved writing this scene: the journey on the back of the bike, the sudden view of the ancient house, the sense of a family and home so very different from her own – messy, slightly bohemian and much more relaxed and accepting than her parents' neat, organised house where her parents are still grieving for her brother Joe. Writing it, and now reading it again, I can feel the warmth and generosity of the family. When I was a teenager, I longed to live in a house like that. I imagined that when I was grown up, I might have a large family and a beautiful old house with a big garden, an orchard, hens; house martins and swallows flying in and out of the eaves . . . And maybe the novel-writing mum (Maddie) is a version of the woman I might have been, given different circumstances! I didn't realise that when I was writing, but I see it more clearly now.

Objects from Bringing the Summer

Many aspects of this story are inspired by 'real' events and objects. Gabes' old scooter bought off eBay is based on my son's first bike (it met a sad end); the place on the river near the weir where people swim and picnic is inspired by a place I know near where I live. All the scenes in Oxford, including the objects in the Pitt Rivers Museum, are closely based on real places and things. I imagined Freya and Gabes' drawings and paintings, but the Winifred Nicholson paintings are real. I love the colours she uses, and her images of windows and windowsills: the borders between 'inside' and 'outside'. Looking through a book about her work (*Winifred Nicholson* by Christopher Andreae, Lund Humphries, 2009) I found the painting 'Dawn Chorus' with its beautiful colours, uplifting and joyful. There are many paintings of sea and landscape which Freya would love, as I do. I think in another life I would like to be a visual artist.

These connections seem to happen as I write: I don't plan it all out, but as I immerse myself in a story all sorts of ideas and images, experiences and memories seem to come to the surface. Many of them I've already written about in my notebooks, as if my subconscious mind knows they are important in some way.

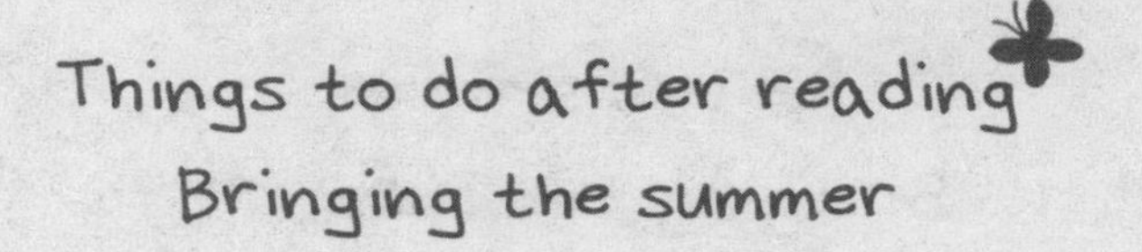

- Swim in a river. (Do all the safety checks first, and never swim by yourself. There are books and websites about wild swimming.)

- Visit Oxford: go to the Pitt Rivers Museum and look for the objects Freya sees, including the gilt bee from Burma, the moss and bark figures from Russia and the old skates and snowshoes. Visit some of the colleges and chapels, and have coffee in the covered market. Take a walk to Port Meadow.

- Read some of John Keats' poems; watch the film *Bright Star* on DVD.

- Draw and paint in a notebook. Look at paintings by the Pre-Raphaelites and Winifred Nicholson.

- Make someone you love an advent calendar: paint all the tiny pictures yourself.

- Next time it snows, go sledging with friends.

- Read *Breathing Underwater* and *Drawing with Light*.

A room of my own

My attic is the place where I can escape to write. It is quiet at the top of the house, and from the skylight windows I can see hills and fields and trees and plenty of sky. It is full of books, some on shelves, others stacked high on the floor. There are piles of paper, boxes of old manuscripts, and photos, postcards, other things that help me to write whatever story I am currently working on. It is very untidy but I know where everything is! A small carved mouse (Toby's mouse from *The Children of Green Knowe*) perches close to my laptop.

JULIA
GREEN
Drawing
with Light